THE GOLDEN APOSTLES

1811: Anne Stacey's guardian, the cold-hearted Sir Emmet Harley, showed the lovely heiress a sketch of some statuettes. He said they were the priceless Golden Apostles, which had been lost for two centuries but miraculously recovered. Soon the statuettes would arrive in Lima, whither Sir Emmet and his party had gone to further Britain's cause in the war against Napoleon. Anne had no inkling that the Golden Apostles would sweep her into a perilous adventure and that, when all seemed lost, there would enter into her life a brave but enigmatic man, to whom she would lose her heart . . .

NARA LAKE

THE GOLDEN APOSTLES

Complete and Unabridged

ULVERSCROFT
Leicester

First published in Great Britain in 1978

First Large Print Edition
published 2000

All characters in this novel are fictitious and
a product of the author's imagination.

Copyright © 1978 by Nara Lake
All rights reserved

British Library CIP Data

Lake, Nara
The Golden Apostles.—Large print ed.—
Ulverscroft large print series: romance
1. Love stories
2. Large type books
I. Title
823.9'14 [F]

ISBN 0–7089–4245–8

Published by
F. A. Thorpe (Publishing)
Anstey, Leicestershire
Set by Words & Graphics Ltd.
Anstey, Leicestershire
Printed and bound in Great Britain by
T. J. International Ltd., Padstow, Cornwall

1

How good it was to be Home again!

Yet, during her unhappy sojourn in the tropics, Anne had forgotten how cool it could be in England during late May, and her muslin dress was far too light for the pale sunlight and chilly breeze as she alighted from the carriage and was escorted indoors by her excited aunt and cousins.

She was tired. Her experiences had left her thin, and although on the voyage from the Indies she had been pampered by the other women passengers, she was still weary with an exhaustion of the soul. Her aunt, her late mother's sister, whom her former guardian Sir Emmet Harley had so often described as a fool, was sufficiently wise to leave Anne to tell her story in her own time. It was enough that the girl had been returned so miraculously, and physically unharmed. She was young, only twenty two, and time would gradually erase her fearful memories.

For the time being, declared Mrs. Bretherton, the main thing was to make Anne presentable again. What a dowdy dress! And her hair! It would have to be trimmed, and arranged into the latest style. Lotions would have to be applied to the fair skin which had been dried out by too much exposure to salt air.

Anne Stacey was an heiress and quite able to afford all these luxuries. Now that she was safely out of the clutches of that extraordinary man, Sir Emmet Harley, said her aunt, she could join in the whirl of balls, routs and entertainments which were the prerogative of a wealthy class untouched by the long war which still growled in Europe.

As it had when Anne had left England, Napoleon's star blazed high above the world. At this time of her return in 1812, the Emperor's Grand Army of nearly half a million men had been assembled in Poland and was marching towards the Russian borders to crush the Tzar and force a back door into the eastern dominions he had so long coveted. Victory over the Russians seemed inevitable, despite the way in which so many of his best troops were bogged down in Spain. This long campaign, with neither the French forces nor the British and their Spanish allies gaining a decisive victory, was referred to by the Emperor as the Spanish Ulcer and was the result of Napoleon placing his brother Joseph upon the Spanish throne.

Anne's first action after the joy and astonished celebrations which greeted her 'return from the dead' was to request that her late father's solicitor visit her. She knew, of course, that Sir Emmet was currently living quietly at his country residence, Whitestairs, recuperating from a tropical illness and his wife's tragic death. Mrs. Bretherton had not minced words when she told her niece about the short letter which she had received from Sir Emmet, curtly informing her that as far as he knew, Anne was dead.

Mr. Bretherton, a member of Parliament, had immediately pressed for more information, but all he could elicit was that Anne had disappeared under the most peculiar circumstances.

'Mr. Bretherton wrote straight away to Anthony,' continued Mrs. Bretherton. 'Oh, my dear, to think that the poor lad believes you to be dead! What a burden, when he is himself in so much danger.'

Anthony was her stepson, and a major in Lord Wellington's army.

'You must write to him yourself! And pray that he was spared in that dreadful battle at Badajoz! So many fine men killed, and not a word about Anthony!'

Anne duly promised, but delayed writing until after she had spoken to the solicitor. She found it incredibly hard to think of what to say to Anthony Bretherton, whom she would have married if Sir Emmet had not intervened.

When she told the solicitor that she wished it made clear to Sir Emmet Harley that she was no longer his ward, having attained her majority some months previously, and that from now on she would manage her own affairs, she was answered by some tut-tutting and raising of eyebrows.

Sir Emmet, she was told, gently but firmly, had administered Miss Stacey's fortune in a manner beyond reproach, and she should consider very carefully whether she herself had the wisdom and experience to cope with such matters.

'Mr. Bretherton, my aunt's husband, shall advise me,' she replied, 'Now, Sir Emmet still has in his possession some jewellery which belonged to my grandmother, and which is now rightly mine. I have made a list of the items.'

How could she tell this good and conservative old gentleman of her suspicions that her former guardian, now a sick and apparently stricken widower, had murdered his own wife? Besides, all she wanted now was a time of peace, an interval in which to repair those scars left on her memory and pride. By burying herself in the ordered trivialities of an English gentlewoman's existence, she could, she hope, erase those nightmare recollections of the events which had commenced on that fine January morning when the Golden Apostles had been borne in triumph towards the great cathedral at Lima.

'As soon as possible,' she continued, as the lawyer swallowed his astonishment at her forthright manner, which he considered quite out of place in a young lady of quality, 'I wish to set up an establishment of my own, a small but comfortable house, and I should be pleased if you set about enquiring as to the availability of suitable properties immediately. Oh, never fear, I shall be properly chaperoned. There are several ladies on my mother's side of the family who would be of suitable age and position.'

The old lawyer sent her a keen look, but he did not attempt to argue. Her mind was plainly made up, but he could be excused for wondering what experiences had firmed and steeled the character of one so young and attractive. There was a blank of many months between Miss Stacey's disappearance and unexpected return, and she was apparently disinclined to talk about that mysterious period.

Yet, within a very short time, Miss Anne Stacey's bizarre experiences would become the subject of a public scandal.

5

It was on the day when news arrived that Major Anthony Bretherton was on his way home from the Peninsula. He had been wounded at Badajoz, said his letter, a bullet in the leg, nothing serious, but a plaguey nuisance, and he was being sent back to England for a spell.

Mrs. Bretherton was beside herself. She was genuinely fond of her stepson, and fate having decreed that the children she had given her husband were girls, she did not resent the fact that the dashing Anthony would inherit most of Mr. Bretherton's considerable estates.

'After all this time, it seems that my dearest wish may come true!' she declared. 'Oh, my dear, you must not be in such a hurry to set up on your own! Who knows, when you leave this house, it may be as a bride.'

Anne was glancing through a list of properties which had been delivered by her solicitor's clerk. Some were obviously impossible, but at least three she considered worthy of her inspection.

'I am not of a mind to marry yet,' she answered, quite serenely.

'But, my dear, you and Anthony were so much in love, and if had not been for that *impossible* man . . . It was not as if Tony were a fortune hunter.'

'We have not seen each other for a considerable time,' replied Anne, slowly, putting aside the list. 'I must have a while to adjust myself.'

As she spoke, there was a light tap on the door, and the Bretherton's butler entered, askance and apologetic at the same time. There were, he said, in a strained whisper, two persons at the door, demanding entry. They were Bow Street Runners, and desired to talk with Miss Stacey.

'Tell them to return when Mr. Bretherton is at home,' said Mrs. Bretherton. 'I cannot imagine what business they could have with Miss Stacey.'

She was to learn soon enough.

The Runners, although greatly in awe of the elegant surroundings in which they found themselves, and with deference softening their rough Cockney voices, made no bones about the purpose of their visit.

They had with them a magistrate's warrant for the arrest of Miss Anne Elizabeth Stacey, sworn out on information rendered by Sir Emmet Harley, baronet, of Whitestairs in the County of Hampshire. The charges were that she had conspired with others to execute certain acts of treason against the realms and subjects of His Majesty, King George the Third.

2

If only . . .

What melancholy words they were.

If only she had been allowed to return Home to England with the Westons. She remembered the morning when that matter had come to a head, so vividly that it seemed to have happened only days before, instead of many months previously.

At about eleven in the morning, Anne had been summoned to see her guardian in his study. This particular room was on the ground floor of the large house, walled from the street in Spanish style, which was Sir Emmet Harley's residence during his stay in Lima. Although it was mid-morning, and a market day, with the consequent traffic and crowds of humans and animals in the streets, the solid masonry muffled noise so effectively that at this moment the loudest sound was the splashing of the fountain in the courtyard about which the house was constructed.

'No,' he stated, after dismissing his secretary, the grey and subdued Mr. Baxter, 'I cannot permit it. You cannot return to England.'

So saying, he took out his snuff box, and proceeded to indulge his taste for the finest and rarest tobacco, brought all the way from London in specially sealed containers, for he trusted none but one particular dealer to blend his snuff.

Sir Emmet Harley was a tall man, and a strikingly handsome one, with brilliant grey eyes set wide apart, a slightly aquiline nose, and a thin-lipped mouth which suggested strength rather than meanness. He was at this time thirty five years of age, something of a dandy without being foppish, and if his well-fitted dark blue coat was just a shade out of style late in this year of 1810, the garment was still a fine example of the best London tailoring. He was very slightly lame, the result of a childhood accident, and went to great pains to conceal this defect, by the cultivation of a slightly sauntering, almost languid, gait.

Anne Lacey, his second cousin and ward, was a slender girl, a little tall perhaps for some preferences, but well able to carry off the slim, high-waisted gowns which had temporarily liberated fashionable European women from the hoops and stays which had been theirs throughout the eighteenth century. On this day, she wore simple muslin, lightly printed with the blue flowers which so admirably complemented her eyes. Her fair hair was tied with a matching ribbon, and with her straight nose, gently curving wide mouth, and good pale skin with just the slightest blush of rose on the cheeks, she was a pretty girl by any standards. Some members of London society had considered her a little insipid, but they had overlooked the firmness which could set her small chin and the flash which sometimes illuminated her cornflower eyes.

However, she might as well have been a log of wood for all the effect she had on the man.

'You will oblige me by remaining in Lima,' he continued. 'There would be gossip of a possibly unpleasant nature if you left so soon after arriving. In addition, I cannot accept the Westons as suitable companions for a young woman of your position in the world.'

She had known all along that to obtain his permission had been a forlorn hope, but it was hard to hide her resentment and disappointment.

'You must know how difficult my life is,' she insisted, 'Inez and myself find it almost impossible to agree upon anything.'

Inez was Lady Harley, Emmet's part-Spanish wife.

'My dear Anne,' he drawled, 'you must cultivate patience. Remember that I control

10

your destiny until you are of age, and that your majority is still eleven months distant. While we are discussing your problem, I must urge you not to encourage that West Indian planter in his attentions to yourself.'

He uttered the last words with a sneer which relegated planters to the lowest social rung.

Her reaction was instant, a short, incredulous laugh.

'Mr. Laurence? I am not encouraging Mr. Laurence.'

'I would point out that the ways of Spanish society are far more rigid and constrained than our own,' he said, as if she had not spoken. 'To ride even a few paces ahead of others in the company of a man not a husband or close relative can cause unfavourable comment.'

She knew that he was referring to the previous morning when, for a few minutes, she and the personable planter had ridden alongside one another whilst six or so members of the tiny British community were out on horseback in the cool hours after dawn.

'Oh, a fig for them!'

The incident had been accidental, but she felt obliged to protest. Yet, at the same time, she was surprised. Emmet, for all his seeming perspicacity when it came to judging others, had not yet realised that Mr. Laurence's interest was directed, not to herself, but to Inez.

'We have the need to consider their opinions on such matters, Anne.'

She was now at a loss, but felt that she had to say something.

'If you feel so strongly about Mr. Laurence, you should not invite him to this house.'

'Unfortunately, we need Mr. Laurence to forward our business in Peru. Now, I trust that you will write a suitable note to the Westons thanking them for their kindliness, but pointing out that you are unable to accept their offer of escort back to Britain.'

So saying, he placed a little snuff, delicately, on the back of his left hand, a white, strong hand, unspoiled by hard work, but powerful enough to manage, with its partner, a team of four horses. This was the end of the interview, and the girl walked from the room without another word, her light sandals tapping on the tiled floor of the cavernous entrance hall as she hurried towards the wide, dark stairs which led to the upper floors of this palatial house built about a courtyard.

How wretched was the whole situation!

After three years of enduring his guardianship, Anne understood that Sir Emmet enjoyed bending others to his will and that he used as a weapon the mistakes and faults of those who were dependent upon him.

Anne's parents had died when she was sixteen, leaving her an heiress of considerable expectations, and ward of her father's only close relative, a cousin. Within a year, he too had died, and despite efforts by her mother's relatives, his son Emmet assumed control of Anne's life. As a child, she had hero-worshipped that clever, ambitious young man who had his eye on one of the more important ambassadorships. Rumour indicated that was the reason why he had married Inez, who, although English by birth, was connected to a powerful Spanish family with influence in both Old and New Worlds. Admittedly, her Roman Catholicism was still a drawback in England, but for Emmet, the match had many advantages, including estates in Spain when the war ended — hopefully with the restoration of the old monarchy.

It was his marriage which had paved the way to Sir Emmet's being chosen for this delicate mission in South America. Napoleon's closure of continental ports to British trade was having desperate results in England's manufacturing regions, causing great hardship amidst humble folk and severely affecting the country's income as a whole. On the other hand, British involvement in the Iberian Peninsula after Napoleon had annexed the Spanish throne on his brother's behalf had led to the promise of new markets. For centuries, the trading rights of Central and South America had been forbidden to outsiders.

Britain was fighting for Spain because she was fighting Napoleon, but Spain was a traditional enemy, and the closed-door policy in the Americas had irritated Britons since the days of Sir Francis Drake. The idea of an independent South America suited British traders down to the ground, but they did not relish the sort of revolution which would drive that huge country into the Napoleonic sphere of influence. At the same time, they had to avoid offending the Spanish royalists who were Britain's allies in the Peninsular campaign.

When Sir Emmet had been chosen as an envoy to Lima, the most important town on the Pacific seaboard, Anne had begged to be permitted to stay in England. There would be few British people in Lima, and she dreaded being imprisoned in the company of her guardian and his wife. Sir Emmet was adamant: she must accompany them. It would, he added, help her to forget that recent foolish episode in her life and allow her time to reflect upon her position in life as a wealthy and well-bred young woman.

The worst of this was, it was partly her own fault.

She had known Anthony Bretherton since her early teens. Three years her senior, he was stepson to her aunt. By most standards, he was eligible, pleasant to look at, from an old family, and with expectations above average. He was on leave from Spain when the cousinly relationship which had formerly existed between the two deepened into love. He was an impetuous young man, and wanted marriage immediately. In love for the first time, she was more than willing to agree, but Sir Emmet stepped in and forbade the match. He had grander plans for his ward. He had himself married for the sake of ambition, and saw no purpose in his attractive ward throwing herself away on a young man who, if he survived the war, would promptly retire into country squireship, perhaps taking over his father's parliamentary seat later in life.

The Brethertons were solid, well-to-do, dutiful Britons. Bretherton senior sat out his sessions in the House of Commons scarcely uttering a word. It was doubtful whether he was on more than nodding acquaintance with any cabinet minister. Whilst he did this, Sir Emmet said sarcastically, his wife dithered about socially in London until it was time to return to their rustic wilderness. Harley made no secret of the fact that he despised the whole family.

Young Captain Bretherton was only briefly dismayed by Sir Emmet's refusal to allow his ward to marry. He immediately arranged an elopement, and Anne, carried away by romance and the thought that she had the right to snatch happiness before Anthony returned to the war, agreed. Lady Harley scented something amiss, and the somewhat harebrained scheme collapsed before it had time to take real shape.

For Sir Emmet Harley, other people were chess pieces to be moved about for one purpose — fulfilment of his own ambitions. For Anne, there had to be a 'great' marriage. To leave her in England, while he worked for his country in Lima, was gambling with this chance. She would, of course, be of age by the time he returned to England, and beyond his power. So, she had to join the baronet's entourage, and never mind her tears and protests whilst her despondent sweetheart sailed back to Portugal and more hard campaigning.

Lima, rebuilt after an earthquake about half a century earlier, was far better laid out and more impressive than the English party had expected. The ruthless conqueror of the Incas, Francisco Pizarro, had chosen the site of his capital with care. Cuzco, the ancient capital, was in the mountains, and too far from the sea for people relying upon ships for trade. It seldom rained in Lima, which was situated upon the banks of a fine river, but the city was cooled by breezes from the ocean, about six miles distant and by winds blowing down from the great snow-clad Cordilleras. With irrigation to provide water for fountains and gardens, the wealthier part of the town was attractive as well as exotic to English eyes. It was small wonder that rich young Creoles — or Americanos, as they preferred to call themselves — were apt to turn up their noses at Old Spain's grubby and cramped towns. The streets of Lima were wide and straight, and the great square was overlooked by a magnificent cathedral rich with treasures. Rather to the surprise of the new arrivals, the climate was not as hot as anticipated, despite the city's proximity to the equator.

A large house near the viceroy's palace

had been leased for the English party, and Sir Emmet lost no time in commencing to feel his way through what turned out to be a tricky maze of local politics. For his wife and ward, there was relief at having arrived safely at their destination after a very long and often dangerous journey, and for a little while, this relief formed something of a bond between them, but they were too different in temperament not to clash.

What had brought matters to a head between Anne and Inez after several strained weeks was the matter of the jewellery. Anne had been left some rather oldfashioned, heavy pieces of considerable value, which she intended to have reset into a more modern style when she came of age. This collection was kept with Sir Emmet's valuables, and she was astonished to learn that it had been brought to Lima. He explained that when they attended certain functions, at the viceregal palace for instance, she would need to wear some jewellery, and although he agreed that most of her inheritance was unsuitable for a young, unmarried woman, perhaps the resetting of some pieces could be arranged here in Lima.

Unfortunately, Inez took a strong fancy to certain items, wearing them constantly, despite owning a valuable collection of her own, and to the extent that Anne suspected that Inez considered them a permanent acquisition. Inez had a rather unfortunate habit of wearing jewellery whether or not the occasion demanded it, and to see her own property thus paraded annoyed Anne immensely.

Perhaps, in less confined circumstances, all this would have been no more than an irritation, but inevitably there was a quarrel, which was taken to Emmet, who was immediately bored by the whole thing. He saw nothing wrong in Inez wearing the trinkets, as he contemptuously described them, for she tired of almost anything so quickly that it was obviously just a temporary fad. He was punctilious in locking the pieces away every night, and as they were not the most valuable items in Anne's inheritance, he saw no need for such an upset. So saying, he returned to the letters he was dictating to his secretary.

The next day, Anne met the Westons, shabby country folk whose commonplace appearance gave little hint of their amazing background. They were quiet, ordinary people who, although lay persons, had bravely undertaken to join a missionary venture at Tahiti. Even their brave spirits had faltered after several years of discouragement, both from the indifference of the natives and outright hostility from visiting seafarers, and with Mrs. Weston's advancing years becoming a burden, they had left for New South Wales on a trading schooner, this being the first leg of the long voyage back to England. A violent storm had blown the vessel far off its course, and when the ship was almost foundering, the desperate survivors had been rescued by a Spanish ship on its way from Manila to Peru.

In former times, their position as heretic missionaries would have been precarious, but changing times — and the war with France — had led to the Westons being kindly treated, along with the other few members of the ship's company. When they had arrived at Peru, they had been amazed to discover that the British government now had sufficient influence there to ensure that they were well looked after until their passage home could be arranged.

'Oh, how I wish I could go home!'

Anne was still young enough to allow her tongue to run away with her, and kindly Mrs. Weston realised the very real unhappiness which lay behind the declaration, and she immediately suggested, shyly, that perhaps Miss Stacey could travel back under the protection of herself and her husband.

Right from the start, there had been very little hope that Emmet would agree, but his refusal was none-the-less hard to bear. Going up to her room on that close December morning after this latest confrontation — and defeat — Anne fumed bitterly at the sheer unfairness of being a woman. The only small comfort she could grasp is that she would be able to entrust letters to the Westons.

Strangely, it was then that the first doubts about marrying Anthony Bretherton crept into her mind. Did she really wish to exchange one master for another? Emmet had interfered, but in spite of that, she had been so sure that she and Anthony would eventually marry. Now the errant idea grew and gained strength even as she walked towards her room. Do I wish to be a cipher for the rest of my life? I am a woman of means, or shall be when I attain my majority. How long does love last? Is it enough to make up for having one's husband command every detail of one's life?

In Anne's room, Christie Waters, her personal maid, was folding her mistress's freshly laundered shifts into a drawer of the big, heavily carved tallboy which was part of the furniture in the bedroom. It was typical of the whole house, solid and dark, and very Spanish.

21

'Well, Christie, we're not going back to England,' Anne said bluntly, going to the long windows which led out on to the upper gallery. 'We've lost our chance and had best resign ourselves to Lima.'

So saying, she pushed open a window, and immediately in rushed the strange exotic noises of this city so removed from the world she and Christie Waters had known. The sounds came in from a distance, but clearly: the vendor's cries, the haunting melody of a strange Indian tune played on a primitive instrument, the braying of mules, the shouts of the muleteers, a rattle of wheels over paved streets, and the pealing of bells from the cathedral. It was noon, the guard was being changed outside the viceregal palace, and Inez would shortly be home, accompanied correctly by her maid, returning from her daily excursion to take mass.

'I'm sorry, Miss Anne,' replied Christie, with considerable feeling. Like her mistress, she had not wished to leave England, though her reasons were mostly based on a deep suspicion of foreign parts. Unfortunately, during the long voyage, Lady Harley's own personal maid had died. On arrival in Lima, she soon acquired a new servant, a mestizo named Rosina Perez, and a mutual dislike flourished betwixt the Peruvian and Christie.

22

Rosina was competent enough, having been trained into the duties of a lady's maid in a wealthy Spanish household. Her appearance was striking, her features being classically Inca, but only lightly olive, and highlighted by large eyes of a peculiar greenish shade. It was soon passed on through the English staff that she was descended from one of the ruffian Pizarro brothers, plunderers of Old Peru, and a well-born Inca woman he had snatched from a convent in pagan, sun-worshipping Cuzco. Whether this tale was a piece of romantic fancy or not, there was no way of telling, but there could be no doubt that it gave Rosina considerable standing amongst other mestizo servants in the neighbourhood.

At the same time, by what Anne saw as a rather unfortunate coincidence, Rosina's brother Francisco was employed as a body servant by none other than Robert Laurence, the West Indian planter who had become so friendly with Lady Harley.

3

Although Sir Emmet Harley sneered at Robert Laurence — and seemed ignorant of the way in which his wife favoured the younger man — Robert Laurence was that day to be a guest at his table for the midday meal.

West Indian born, Laurence was of part-Spanish extraction like Lady Harley, and had recently come from Jamaica to Peru, where he had inherited property. The long wars since the French Revolution had prevented his entry into the country until that time. It was only a brief while before Sir Emmet's own arrival that he had made the journey to Lima in order to claim his inheritance, which, he said, he intended to sell so that he could invest the money in improving his West Indian property.

He was a good-looking man of twenty seven, slender, and with dark hair and eyes without being swarthy. He had the assured air of one whose conquests had been many, and although his manners were good, there was about him a conceit which Anne found almost repellant, especially when he flirted with her so determinedly. With Inez, he was immediately on surer ground, being able to speak Spanish as fluently as herself, and Lady Harley, bored and childless after five years of loveless marriage, was ready for just such a distraction as the planter offered.

Despite all this, Robert Laurence was still an invaluable assistant in forwarding British influence in this remote country which could provide the bullion, in return for manufactured goods, which the English needed so desperately to finance their war against Napoleon Bonaparte. Best of all, he could talk to the young upper-class Peruvians as one Americano to another, sharing with them the common bond of having been born in the New World. Thus, despite Sir Emmet's antipathy, Robert Laurence was a frequent visitor to the house, where he spent much time discussing the latest rumours and developments with the baronet and his secretary behind the closed doors of Harley's study.

Before her unhappy and fruitless interview with her guardian, Anne had changed for the occasion of the midday meal, but now, she noticed with annoyance, that the frill at her hemline was torn. As Christie helped her change, and sought about for the right ribbon to thread through her mistress's fair curls, the maid stated with a sniff of disapproval that there were things going on in this house which should not be, and she wished to heaven that they were leaving.

'Christie,' said Anne sharply, 'I shall not have you repeating servants' gossip to me!'

Christie shrugged. In her middle twenties, she was a full-bosomed, rosy-cheeked woman at the height of her looks, who tended at times to impertinence. However, she was both hard-working and competent, but every so often she needed to be reprimanded.

Christie found the ribbon to replace the one which matched the blue-patterned gown, and bound it deftly into place. In the looking-glass Anne could see that the other's full lips were set sulkily.

'I wish very much that we were leaving,' she added, in a gentler tone of voice. 'However, it's not to be, and we must be patient. Our stay is not forever.'

'I don't like it,' grumbled Christie, with a final touch of the comb. 'I don't like it at all, and there's those who are getting ideas.'

Then she saw by the glint in Anne's eyes that she best say no more.

The meal passed pleasantly. Emmet made no reference to the angry interlude between himself and Anne which had taken place earlier, and Mr. Laurence talked lightly

26

and amiably on harmless topics, giving no indication of the way matters had developed between himself and his host's wife. Eventually, the two women retired for the siesta. Inez had adapted quickly to local customs, which suited her indolent nature. Every afternoon she lay down, to be fanned by Rosina until she dozed off.

A vigorous country upbringing had led Anne to believe that daylight hours should not be wasted, but she felt the humid warmth of Lima's afternoons badly, and as a result, was content to spend that time indoors. After the rebuff of the morning, she felt that she could not bear to tell the kindly Westons to their faces that she would not be able to travel under their chaperonage. She wrote a letter, explaining that her guardian felt it best that she should remain under his direct care for the time being. It read calmly and sensibly, and gave no hint of the anger she felt against the cold-natured and ambitious man.

She thought, I shall ask Mr. Laurence to deliver it, as he must pass by their lodgings on his way to his own.

The house was so quiet that she could hear the raised and angry voices behind the heavily carved door to Sir Emmet's study, although she could not distinguish words deadened by solid dark panels.

The door was opened, abruptly, whilst Anne stood irresolute at the base of the stairs.

'Mr. Laurence, I must remind you that you are a Briton and that your country is fighting for its life against the most powerful, and the most evil tyrant the world has ever seen. The gold and silver Peru can exchange for British goods is urgently needed. It is of the greatest importance that our mission here is completed as quickly as possible.'

Robert Laurence came out in a whirl of fury, curiously un-English, but when he saw Anne, he paused and treated her to that careless smile, so often the tool of the lady-killer, although his eyes were snapping with rage. She instantly realised that to request that he deliver her letter to the Westons would be indiscreet. Therefore, she acknowledged his smile with a cool nod, and the man snatched his hat from the sleepy Indian servant who emerged from a sort of closet near the main door.

'You wished to see me?'

Apparently, Sir Emmet was not going to extend to the visitor the courtesy of seeing him across the courtyard to the street door, but he made a gesture to Anne that she herself should enter the study.

She was embarrassed and diffident, not wishing to be embroiled in the quarrel, which she feared could be over Laurence's involvement with Lady Harley.

'I've a letter for the Westons,' she explained, in a low voice. 'I had hoped to send one of the servants with it.'

He held out his hand for the letter.

'I can arrange the matter myself,' she said, stiffly.

'Not until after the siesta,' he reminded her. 'I've letters to be delivered, too, and yours can go with them. I assume that you are following my wishes, and that you have written to the Westons telling them that you will not be leaving Lima?'

She said nothing, and he continued talking, without referring to that disagreement with Laurence which had sent the planter hurrying from the house.

'No guardian with a sense of responsibility would have yielded. I would be failing in my duty to your parents, God rest their souls, if I acted otherwise.'

How she loathed him when he spoke thus! If he had been of a warmer and less calculating nature, she might have believed in his solicitude.

'You must not regret Major Bretherton. He interested you because you were young and inexperienced, and a little dazzled by his quick promotion on the field of battle. One day, Anne, there will be a great marriage for you.'

'To an old man, or a worn-out rake, with a title and the right amount of influence with the Prime Minister,' she retorted.

'I doubt it. The man who chooses you, my dear ward, will have his work cut out to tame you, and no old man could do that. But I do not despair of finding the correct husband for you.'

She stared back at him with all that special hatred which so often surpasses that felt for persons outside the blood tie. Just as she felt that she could not stand another second of his company, he became unexpectedly amiable.

'There is something of the greatest importance to our mission here in Lima which I must discuss with you,' he said, quite pleasantly. 'Much of your discontent, Anne, is due to boredom. You are making too much of trivialities. I know that this town is dull and limited for a young woman of your spirit and intelligence, but you could so easily further our cause in this country.'

Despite herself, she felt a quickening of interest. Whatever his faults, no one could ever doubt Sir Emmet Harley's intense patriotism. He was ambitious for his own ends, but he could have found an easier way to further them than by coming to this faraway and alien land.

'Something quite remarkable has occurred, and we must use it to help stabilise our position in South America.'

So saying, he crossed to his desk and took from the top a sheet of stiff paper, which he handed to her. She could only look down blankly at the crudely drawn sketches.

'But what are these?' she asked. 'They look like statues. Are they Inca idols?'

The room was dim, with the shutters half closed, and she crossed to the long window opening out on to the shadowed lower gallery. Robert Laurence had not left, but was standing by the street door, his face turned upwards towards Inez's room. The girl, hoping that Sir Emmet would not see, moved away quickly and handed the paper back to her guardian.

'They do represent statues, or perhaps statuettes would be a better description. To good Protestants like ourselves, Anne, they could be described as idols, but they are imagined likenesses of the twelve apostles, and they are made of solid gold and embellished with precious stones.'

31

'You mean, like the apostles already in the cathedral?'

'Yes. In fact, they are the originals. The ones you have seen were made to replace these.'

As he enlarged, she listened in fascination. During the construction of the present cathedral, nearly two centuries earlier, there had been found in the high Andes a rich cache of Inca treasure overlooked during the earlier looting when the Pizarro brothers and their cohorts had rampaged through the old empire. This treasure had taken the form of twelve golden statuettes of the ancient gods, the work of Inca craftsmen. The priest who had made the discovery had arranged to have the idols recast into the likenesses of Christ's disciples with St. Matthias, as was the usual custom, being substituted for Judas. The treasure had been laden on to pack llamas, and the long journey commenced along the lofty and perilous trails to Cuzco as the first stage of the long and arduous way to Lima.

Somewhere, before the party reached Cuzco, the entire contingent of men and beasts, and the good priest, had vanished. The Indians had muttered that the gods had avenged themselves upon the sacrilegious, but the hard-headed Spaniards suspected bandits. Later, another set of apostles had been cast, these being the ones to be seen in the cathedral to that day.

Two months previously, about the time of the arrival of Sir Emmet Harley and his party in Lima, there had been a violent earthquake between Cuzco and the silver mining city of Potiso. Hundreds of poor Indians were said to have perished, but such was the isolation of the area, that only now had news of the disaster reached the Viceroy here in Lima. Along with the tragic tidings came the story of an astonishing event.

A cave, long sealed by a landslide, had been exposed, and inside, where the owners had died whilst sheltering from a storm, were the mummified remains of Father Pedro, crucifix still clutched in skeletal fingers, and all his party. The dry airlessness of the tomb had preserved both the bodies and the leather boxes which had held the statutes, and when these latter were opened by the awestruck discoverers of this macabre scene, the jewelled contents gleamed and glowed with an unearthly radiance which made those poor peasants believe that they were in the presence of a miracle.

The statuettes were taken to a remote village, awaiting instructions from the Viceroy, for, fortunately, that humble band of men who made the discovery were both honest and devout, and as well still owed their allegiance to Peru, and not to the breakaway province in the southeast.

Within hours of the news reaching Lima, the whole population, Spaniard, mestizo and Indian, was excited. Was this discovery a sign of Divine intervention into men's affairs?

There were many who were sure that it was indeed a sign and they read it according to their own beliefs and desires. The ultra-conservative *gente-distinguida*, comprising the wealthy and professional Creole families, felt that the find was a blessing upon the Spanish royal house, and that their allegiance must remain firmly with the junta supporting Prince Ferdinand, who had been deposed by the abdication of his senile father, Charles the Fourth, in favour of Joseph Bonaparte. For them, faith and crown remained inseparable.

On the other hand, there was a growing proportion of Americanos who disliked both the ancient aristocracy of Spain and the lack of understanding with which Peninsular Spaniards treated those born in the colonies. Ambitious young men of good family here in Peru had long resented the way in which plum positions invariably went to new arrivals from the old country, and latterly, they were objecting to orders from the junta which had rallied Spain against Napoleon. Members of the junta, they said, were upstarts, not royalty, and the Americanos would be just as well off ruling themselves. To this part of the population, the rediscovery of the Golden Apostles was symbolic of finding freedom.

Then there were the true revolutionaries, many of them part Indian, who wanted a complete change, and a casting aside of the Spanish system for good. They were ready to accept Napoleon's domination of Old Spain if it meant the end to Spanish domination and the tiresome creakings of a corrupt bureaucracy.

On the eastern seaboard of the huge South American continent, Buenos Aires, the most European of the colonial cities, had been the scene of one upset after another since the premature British invasion back in 1806. In the Vice-royalty of Peru, there had already been revolts against Lima's rule down south in Chile, and in the area about remote La Paz, landlocked high in the Andes. Spanish South America was straining itself to the breaking point, just as the great faults beneath the mountains moved and chafed until the earth was cracked violently open.

'So you see, my dear Anne,' said Sir Emmet Harley, concluding this explanation, 'that it behoves us to persuade our Peruvian friends that the discovery of the Apostles is a true sign that Bonaparte shall be driven from Spain and ultimately defeated.'

'We have precious little with which to persuade them,' she replied, ruefully. 'We've had great victories at sea, but precious few on land.'

'Our sea victories may in the end be worth more than Bonaparte's on the land,' remarked the other. 'Provided we can find markets to take the place of those we've lost on the Continent so that our country can afford to continue fighting! For the present, though, I trust that you and Lady Harley will try to patch up your differences. There will be a round of celebrations when the Apostles finally reach Lima, and by joining in them at every opportunity, we may be able to advance our own cause. Unhappily, Mr. Laurence has chosen this time to go north to his properties. Still, I think we can manage without him.'

He made no further reference to the quarrel which had taken place between himself and the West Indian planter, but there was a sharpness to his tone which made it clear that he considered Mr. Laurence's departure at this time as little short of a dereliction of duty.

4

Being a wealthy young woman in her own right, Anne Stacey was spared the necessity of having to share one of the dreadful common apartments in Newgate Prison. For her, there was the privilege of a private room, hastily furnished into some comfort with odds and ends from her aunt's London house. On the way, she had been led through a common apartment, and had been appalled and sickened by the sheer squalor and misery of the scene. Prostitutes, old hags, children, and quite decent looking women were mixed in indiscriminately. Some were in rags, some in flash finery, and some were drunk. They had all stopped whatever it was they were doing as she passed, and one old crone pointed at her.

' 'Tis Old Boney's mort!' she screeched.

This was the first intimation Anne had of just how quickly news could spread through a prison. Already, she had been identified as a traitor to her country.

Mr. Bretherton had been hastily summoned from the House of Commons by his distraught wife, and he set about instantly to discover how this could happen to a member of his family. The elderly solicitor who had watched over the Stacey family affairs for so many years was quite plainly out of his depth in this, and Mr. Bretherton immediately sought the best legal advice available.

He also picked up some gossip about Sir Emmet Harley which was mildly enlightening, if not altogether explanatory.

'Fellow came home more or less in disgrace,' he told Anne when he visited her. 'No wonder he skulked off to Whitestairs. Can't quite get to the bottom of it, but it seems he was hoping poor old Percival would stick up for him. They'd been friendly, y'know. Perceval gave him this mission to Peru.'

(Spencer Perceval, Prime Minister of England, had been shot dead by a demented bankrupt in the lobby of the House of Commons during May of that same year.)

'No one seems to know what went wrong for Harley,' continued Mr. Bretherton, wiping his face with a handkerchief. The room was stuffy in the summer warmth, and slightly noisome with prison smells. 'Now, me girl, you're to put all your thoughts in order. I've found the man to put things to rights. I'm warning you, he's the look of a regular rakehell, but he's the smartest lawyer in London. Trust him.'

Anne held out her hand to the bluff country squire who seemed so out of place in these confined surroundings.

'Thank you,' she said, her blue eyes filling with tears. 'Thank you for believing in my innocence.' Her voice faltered. 'My story is so strange . . . and there is no one left to say that it is true.'

Mr. Bretherton grasped her hand briefly.

'The whole thing is a stupid farrago. The Harleys were always a trifle touched,' he declared, gruffly.

Then she was alone.

So much for the hope that she would be able to spend the rest of her life as if those blank months had never been. She had been so determined to blot out the terrors — and the brief sweetness — of her memories, but tomorrow she would have to tell them to a stranger. On her way back to England, she had resolved that she would not think of *him* again. Of course, it was a somewhat useless resolution, because he had the oddest habit of turning up in dreams, of appearing to pass in the street, or in a carriage travelling in the opposite direction, only, of course, to be someone else entirely. It would all fade in time if she gave it no encouragement.

39

One day, when Anthony returned from the war, she would marry him, and settle down happily without an errant thought of a lanky young man with lively brown eyes and more courage than she had ever imagined.

If she were still alive she would marry Anthony.

Were traitors still drawn and quartered?

She must not think thus. She must work out a starting point for her story.

During the weeks between the arrival of the news about the rediscovery of the Golden Apostles, and the day when the relics were borne so triumphantly into Lima, there had been a pleasant and busy interval. For Sir Emmet, there were some setbacks as he made certain basic conclusions. Here, in Latin America, nothing hurried. There were sharpminded merchants in Lima, eager to make money, but Creole officialdom, rooted so often in the minor Spanish nobility, took a maddeningly slow and apathetic view of the business dealings it considered far beneath its dignity.

Sir Emmet Harley also came face to face with a disturbing fact. South America was not the vast market of British imagination. It was certainly a source of gold and silver and precious stones, but except for the small ruling class, the bulk of its people were too poor to buy manufactured goods. It was little wonder that the baronet was often short-tempered, even with his secretary, the patient and discreet Mr. Baxter.

Socially, however, success was greeting the British party. The carnival feeling, which swept the city as the Apostles were moved slowly from town to town to receive the adulation of local people, had the important result of unlocking the reserve with which many important Peruvians had treated the British delegation. Never mind that the British army had fought so hard on their behalf in Spain — these newcomers were English and Protestant, traditional foes for centuries.

In retrospect, those weeks seemed unreal. Dashing young Americanos competed for a few minutes of Anne's time, and she would have been an unusual young lady if she had not enjoyed every moment of this popularity. On the sidelines, Sir Emmet watched shrewdly, assessing each and every young man's value as an ally. She took Spanish lessons, and enjoyed the innocent reciprocation of testing her small knowledge against the halting English of her admirers.

'I'm glad now that we didn't go,' said Anne one forenoon, as Christie hooked the back of her gown.

'H'm.' Christie, gleaming dark curls just visible under her cap, still did not like Lima. 'They're certainly making a great to-do over a lot of heathen idols.'

Anne laughed.

'You'd best not say that outside the house. Someone might understand you!'

'I don't like going outside. All those heathen Indians in their queer clothes. As for that Rosina! She's a witch. I'm sure of it.'

'Nonsense.'

She made light of it, but she did not much care for Rosina herself, although there was no doubt that Inez found the Peruvian to her liking as a servant.

'I was lookin' out of a window yesterday, and I saw Rosina by the door going out into the side lane. There was an old Indian woman there, and she was giving something to Rosina. We'd best watch out, Miss Anne, or she'll poison the lot of us.'

This was said so vehemently that Anne was startled.

'Christie,' she said, quite sharply, 'you mustn't let your fancies run away with you like that. Rosina is quite entitled to talk to her friends. The old woman may even have been her mother.'

Though she made light of it, she determined

to mention the incident to Sir Emmet if the chance occurred. He was always very much above servants' tittle-tattle, but Christie was not a fool, and Anne suspected that she may have had a reason for saying such things.

Still, there was too much else happening to dwell on the behaviour of Lady Harley's abigail. Lady Harley herself was not really entering into their social life with much joy. She had been downcast ever since Robert Laurence had left so abruptly to pursue his own private interests. Now, she began to be actively jealous of her husband's lovely ward, whose blonde prettiness had a sensational impact upon the men, unmarried or not, of Lima's exclusive class. In contrast, Inez was sallow, plump and ordinary, and to her annoyance, found herself placed amidst the duennas who overlooked the young girls. Anne felt sorry for her, without liking her. Robert Laurence's admiration had meant so much to her, after years of her husband's indifference.

Then, ten days after Christmas, Robert Laurence returned, without warning. He simply sauntered in one day whilst the Harleys and Anne were eating a late breakfast, seated at the table which had been brought out into the courtyard.

He was a little thinner, presumably because travelling about the Peruvian countryside was a very strenuous affair, very sure of himself, and as handsome as ever. No one was more startled than Inez, who had been languid, bored and still very much irritated by the way in which Anne had been so admired and fussed over at the previous night's entertainment.

'Oh, so you're back,' said Sir Emmet, for all the world as if the other man had been delayed on a short errand. 'And your business was brought to a successful conclusion, I trust?'

'Yes, it was, sir. There are still a few loose ends, but everything went forward far better than I expected, and as well, I was fortunate enough to be able to return by sea.'

'You will take tea? Coffee?'

Inez sounded too eager for such an ordinary invitation, and Anne wondered anew how it was that Sir Emmet did not seem to notice his wife's infatuation for Robert Laurence. She was not so innocent as to be unaware that the partners in loveless marriages did seek solace elsewhere, but Inez's adoration fairly blazed out of her dark eyes.

'I have breakfasted, thank you.'

44

Inez may have been guilty of forgetting her discretion in her joy at Laurence's return, but his attention was directed to Anne.

'I have already heard, Miss Stacey, that you have taken the masculine hearts of Lima by storm,' he smiled.

'I fear,' said Anne, lightly, 'that there is an element of novelty in my success.'

Sir Emmet intersposed smoothly. He wished to know whether Mr. Laurence had anything of particular interest to impart, and suggested that they withdraw to his study.

For a few moments after the men had left the courtyard, Inez continued her half-finished meal. Then, suddenly, she arose, and after treating Anne to a look of savage anger, flounced away into the interior of the house. A short time later, Anne heard her crying out in Spanish to Rosina. Anne understood enough to follow the gist.

'We shall go out! Immediately! Anywhere to be away from this wretched house!'

By this time, the Golden Apostles had reached the very outskirts of Lima, and were being kept, under the strongest guard, in a small church. Tomorrow would be a holiday, commencing with a religious procession through the city's main streets. This would be climaxed by a service of thanksgiving in the great cathedral, to be followed by public festivities.

It was expected that many thousands would gather to see the statuettes carried into the cathedral, and a service to complement that being read within would be held before the main doors of the great edifice.

Sir Emmet Harley had already delicately sounded out opinion as to what would be the eventual fate of the statuettes. As the cathedral already held similar treasures, would the long-lost Apostles be kept in Peru? A realist, he saw the images for what they were, the gold so badly needed by his country to assist in the war against Napoleon. He could not, of course, even begin to suggest this, but he understood that the Viceroy was also grappling with this delicate problem. More than any other man in Peru, that dignitary wished to see the rightful king back on the Spanish throne. Aware of the republican mutterings in certain clubs and taverns, he was anxious to protect his own position.

The problem of what was to become of the statuettes would be solved, however, in a way which was expected by none but the conspirators involved.

By the same means, Anne Stacey's easy and protected existence would be shattered

46

into a thousand pieces, and although the time would come when she would try to restore it into a resemblance of what it had been, her life — and herself — would be forever changed.

5

Sir Emmet Harley, his wife and ward had places reserved for them in the cathedral. The actual ceremony was not expected to commence until ten o'clock, but it would be necessary, because of the crowds which had been streaming into the city since dawn, to leave the house no later than nine. It was a fine, hot morning, hazy and very still.

'A lot of fuss over heathenish idols,' Christie said, as she helped Anne dress.

'But you will go out to see the procession?'

Anne suspected that nothing would keep Christie Waters away from the spectacle of brightly uniformed soldiers, the contrastingly sombre priests, monks and nuns, all marching beneath the gorgeous religious banners held high in honour of the Golden Apostles.

'They say they're bringing the bones of that priest who was buried with the statues,' continued Christie, with a sort of relish. 'Holy relics, they call them. Not the sort of thing I'd want to see, Miss Anne.'

Anne smiled. Despite the growing heat, she was in a state of anticipation. Afterwards, she would write to Anthony, describing the scenes she would witness today. The letter would take months to reach him. As so often when she thought of Anthony, she felt a little guilty, for not being in love as much as before. He was a soldier, fighting in a bitter campaign, and deserved her loyalty. When they met again, she would realise that her doubts had been foolish, and they would marry. For the present, she must fight against any schemes Sir Emmet might hatch to arrange a wedding for her.

At this point, there was a tap on the door, which Christie answered.

'It's that Rosina,' she said, in some disgust. 'I can't make out her gibberish.'

'I'll talk to her.'

It took some moments to grasp the meaning of the rush of words, but when she finally understood, Anne felt both anger and disbelief.

In an hour's time, Sir Emmet and his small party would be taking their places alongside other important Britons inside the cathedral, but Inez would not be there, for Inez was eloping with Mr. Robert Laurence.

Lady Harley had already gone to Mr. Laurence's house, and they would be away before noon, for there was a ship ready to sail at Callao, the port of Lima.

Later, Anne knew that she should have

paused before acting as she did. Her guardian was in his study, doing some work with his secretary before leaving. The sensible course would have been to have gone straight to him and relayed Rosina's story, but with Rosina standing there, her face impassive and her strange eyes downcast, she could only think of the disgrace which would be visited upon all the British contingent. She forgot her own disagreements with her guardian, and thought only of his patriotism and his very real endeavours in his country's cause.

Robert Laurence's lodgings were no more than five minutes' walk away. In her faltering Spanish, she instructed Rosina to tell no one, and then, ordering the startled Christie to accompany her, she hastily donned her bonnet before hurrying down to a side door which opened directly on to the street.

'It's none of our affair,' said Christie, almost running to keep up with her anxious mistress.

'Mr. Laurence might listen to me.'

'H'm. He's a sly one, he is.'

No use reprimanding Christie, for it was true.

'We must try. There will be a scandal which will make us all ridiculous.'

Robert Laurence rented the upper storey of a fairly large house, the dwelling of a formerly wealthy widow. This colonial aristocrat was in her way the victim of a prime weakness of the Spanish Peruvians, which was to live in the comfort of their well-laid out cities rather than out on the country estates. It seemed only natural to mortgage the estates in order to keep up a standard of luxury in town. That was what land was for, but the shrewd merchants, often newly arrived from Spain and without the same feeling, did not quite agree. Foreclosure was inevitable, and a proud line going back to the conquistadors was reduced to that worst of all penury, genteel poverty.

An outside staircase had been constructed to give privacy to both the owner and tenant, and this was indicated by the ancient servant at the main door leading into the street. Like everyone else, the greyhead was eager to be off to see the procession, and indeed, faintly in the distance, could be heard chanting and cheers.

Christie stopped still in her tracks.

'They're coming,' she said. 'We must go back and tell Sir Emmet. He'll be ready to leave now.'

'No, I must try. I cannot go up there alone. You must come with me. Lady Harley may be foolish enough to visit a man's lodgings without a duenna, but I am not.'

So saying, Anne lifted her hem slightly and ran upstairs, closely followed by the disapproving and unwilling Christie. She knocked briskly.

'There's no one here,' said Christie sullenly, anxious to leave before they were involved in a scene. 'And it's not our affair, Miss Anne.'

'I can hear someone moving about. And keep your comments to yourself, Christie!'

Anne rapped again, with unladylike force, and the door opened, slowly, barely an inch at a time.

'Mr. Laurence! If Lady Harley is here, I beg you to have some sense of decency. You are dragging all of us into disrepute by your behaviour.'

He was dishevelled, still in his shirtsleeves, and with some disbelief, she saw the blood staining the embroidered whiteness.

'What has happened?'

At first, he seemed too stunned to reply, and shook his head several times before recovering himself.

'Go,' he said thickly. 'Please go.'

This door gave on to a room which combined the offices of entrance hall and reception room, and although he tried to block her view, she saw Inez sprawled on the floor.

'What has happened?'

She had not thought of peril, of horror, just an unthinking curiosity.

'Don't!' He pushed at her, but she was too quick, and slipped past him to kneel besides Lady Harley. Lady Harley wore a light, puff-sleeved gown with a drifting panel from the back shoulders, soft and silky in the shade called eau de nil.

It was brand new, having been copied from an imported fashion plate here in Lima, to Lady Harley's instructions, for although part Spanish herself, Inez found the styles favoured by the local women stiff and oldfashioned.

She's not wearing any jewellery, thought Anne, in that strange reflex of thought which sometimes comes with disaster. In the end, when she intended to elope, she did not take any of either Emmet's or my jewellery.

Anne had seen death before, but not violent death. Inez's chubby face was now permanently set in an expression of frantic surprise. She had been shot in the heart — Anne supposed that the wound was caused by a ball — and now, turning, she saw the pistol in Robert Laurence's hand.

'You killed her!' She was frightened, and heard Christie sobbing.

'No! She killed herself. You must believe

me. She was like that when I came in. I took the gun from her hand.'

'Inez would not kill herself. She is — was — too devout.'

'I . . . ' Robert Laurence seemed suddenly futile and rather helpless. 'You must believe me. I don't understand why, but she killed herself. We were to meet here, but I was a little late.'

'You were eloping together. I know that she planned to go away with you.'

There they were, thought the older, seasoned Anne, as she endured that first night in Newgate, talking it over like two people discussing the weather. And all the while, Inez's lifeblood congealed and the great bells of the cathedral, no more than a few hundred yards distant, thundered out their pealing message of celebration as the procession moved slowly towards the crowded plaza.

'We'd best fetch the master,' said Christie, tugging at Anne's arm.

'No!' Robert Laurence was recovering himself. 'No, you're going to stay here. I'm not going to take the blame for something I didn't do. I told you — she was dead when I came in. I held her to me for a moment. That's how I came to have blood on my shirt. Now I'm going to lock you both in my bedchamber.'

He pointed the pistol at the two young women, who had drawn close together.

'Is that loaded?' Anne had the notion that she must keep talking.

'Stop arguing!' He was becoming very excited. 'Now, both of you, into the other room'

'Please,' sobbed Christie, 'we've done nothing to you, Mr. Laurence. Please let us go.'

'I don't think that the pistol is loaded,' said Anne. 'It has already been fired. We're leaving, Mr. Laurence.'

'Don't be stupid.' But he was uncertain.

'You cannot escape. Lady Harley's maid, Rosina, knows that we are here.'

'Rosina?' he asked, blankly. Then: 'Oh, the fool! I made her promise to tell no one.'

It was not quite clear whether he was referring to Inez or to the mestizo. Minutes were slipping by as the bells pounded endlessly, and Anne knew that the Harley party should have been at the cathedral by now. She guessed that, as the carriage waited, Sir Emmet would be searching for his womenfolk, angry and puzzled.

In that upstairs room, there was stalemate. Neither of the women could be sure that the pistol was indeed harmless, and Laurence had no intention of letting them go.

Then the bells stopped.

What had happened? People were screaming, shots were being fired, and somewhere a cannon boomed. Closer at hand, footsteps thudded up the outside stairs, and the door was thrown open.

He was a very tall man, and he carried a pistol and a sword. That is what Anne noticed in the first confused, puzzled second as he entered.

'What the devil's going on here?' He took in the whole scene at a glance. 'You were to be waiting at the corner. Now who are these, and her?'

He was nodding towards Anne and Christie, and then at the dead woman on the floor.

'Oh damn explanations!' he exploded, before anyone could utter a sound. 'Come on, man! There's no time to lose. The dagoes'll be over their shock any moment.'

But as he spoke, he stared at Anne, taking in her expensive attire, her whole air of wealth and breeding.

'Who's this?' he snapped.

Laurence, still unnerved, managed to stammer out that she was ward to Sir Emmet Harley.

'Bring her. A hostage'll be handy. Now

hurry. Never mind the dead woman. You can explain later.'

Christie, in contrast to her tears and fright of a few minutes earlier, now found a reservoir of courage, and stepped in front of Anne.

'You'll not take her!' she cried. 'You're bad, wicked men, both of you and I'll . . . '

Her words were cut short by the tall man's harsh laughter.

'We'll take both of you!' he announced, and seized Christie's right arm. She immediately screamed and began kicking at him, but just as quickly his apparent good humour vanished and he held his pistol against her temple.

'Come along, both of you! And you too, Rob.'

They scrambled down the stairs. Even after eighteen months, Anne could recall vividly the staring eyes in a haughty old face as they passed the black-clad and mantillaed widow who owned the house. She stood with her old servant, both of them equally speechless with fright as the two men hustled Anne and Christie across the courtyard out into the street.

In the short time since Anne and Christie had gone into that house, the scene in the street had changed entirely. Gone was the atmosphere of fiesta, with people in their best clothes taking a short cut to vantage points near the plaza. The great bells began ringing again, a tocsin and a summons instead of a celebration. A woman knelt by the inert figure of a man, screaming hysterically, shots still were fired intermittently, and many horses clattered along cobbled thoroughfares from the great square of Lima.

Anne, pushed along at pistol point, glimpsed some of the horsemen, tough, ragged, swarthy men with no fear for their own safety and less regard for the lives of others.

'Come on, come on. We must be at Callao before the soldiers gather up their senses.'

There was a coach at the kerb of the main road leading out of Lima to Callao. It was a grand, well-sprung, well-varnished vehicle, commandeered illegally from its owner, and with good horses at the ready. There was a mulatto on the driver's seat, not wearing the livery of a great family, but clad in the garments of a seafarer. As the four bundled inside, the girls protesting, a whip was cracked and the splendidly matched horses bounded forward.

Outside, Anne glimpsed almost empty streets. A few Indians, bewildered, unused

58

to the city at any time, crouched wherever they could find some sort of shelter from the disaster, but nearly all of the crowd which had gathered to watch the procession had dispersed to safety.

'Mr. Laurence!' Anne tried hard to make her voice decisive, but she was painfully aware of the tremble. 'Where are you taking us?'

Laurence did not reply. He was huddled into one corner, his skin greyish, his whole aspect that of a man who had completely lost command over a situation.

'Ma'am,' said the tall man, 'you deserve an explanation.'

She realised now that his accent was a little strange, being tempered with a Yankee twang.

'I'm Captain Peter Ducaine, master and owner of *The Eagle*. Helped by Mr. Laurence's friends, ma'am, we've just caused the biggest stir since Henry Morgan sacked the Spanish Main.' He began to laugh again, that harsh, almost crazy laugh which came from deep down, and which she would always remember, even when his features became hazy with the passage of time.

For the first time, she began to study his appearance, to see him as something except a tall menace. Captain Ducaine was perhaps thirty years of age, though, having the weathered skin typical of seafaring men, it was hard to tell exactly how old he was. He was past six feet tall, and broad across the shoulders, not with the somewhat effete good build of Sir Emmet Harley, but with the toughened muscles of a man who had relied upon his strength since childhood.

He was not at all badlooking, in a rakish fashion, with fair curly hair under a wide-brimmed, finely woven straw hat decorated with coloured ribbons, sharp grey eyes, a fairly large nose, and reasonably good teeth exposed between well-curved lips. For the occasion, he wore shore clothes, unremarkable except for the red silk sash under his coat, into which he now thrust his pistol. The sword, which was Spanish, and which he had snatched from a soldier, he put down on the floor of the coach, having no further use for it.

Christie let out a little squeak, and lifted her feet as if afraid of being cut, showing her ankles, and he laughed again.

'What happened to our first hostage?' he asked the other man. 'I thought we were to have the lady of the British envoy.'

Robert Laurence made a choking noise in his throat.

'Oh, you cared for her, did you? And at the last, she refused to come? And you quarrelled?'

'I didn't touch her.' The words came out of the depths of agony. 'I found her dead. For God's sake, Ducaine, let these women go. They're no good to us.'

'But they are. This ward of Sir Emmet Harley's is as useful as his wife would have been. Any fool can see that she's a lady of quality, so refined, and so elegant. If we're unlucky enough to be overhauled by a British man-o'-war, we'll trade her for our freedom — and the Golden Apostles.'

For the first time, some sense entered this nightmare.

'The Apostles?' The two words jerked from Anne's throat. 'You've stolen the Apostles?'

Captain Ducaine leaned back comfortably in his seat, but one hand hovered at the ready over the butt of his pistol.

'Yes. In a few minutes they'll be safely on board *The Eagle*, and that mad revolutionary leader you found for us, Rob, 'll be fuming on the quay as he watches us up anchor and sail out into the Pacific.'

It began to fit together. Robert Laurence had not been away visiting his estates, or at

61

least, that was not the only purpose of his absence from Lima. He had been helping to organise this daring raid, at the behest of the thoroughly wicked and unscrupulous man who sat opposite Anne.

6

When Anne, recounting her tale to the eminent lawyer who was to undertake her defence, reached her description of the way in which she had been kidnapped, he interrupted her gently. Had, he asked, this abduction been with her consent? She denied it furiously, but in giving his own version of the story to the Crown, Sir Emmet had been thorough and convincing. He had sworn that his ward, embroiled in an affaire with the traitor Robert Laurence, had fled with her lover after he had killed Inez, who had tried vainly to prevent their defection.

'You know, of course, that it will be your word against that of Sir Emmet Harley?'

Tightlipped, her eyes shadowed in a pale face, she nodded, and then, almost casually, he dealt the harshest blow to her hopes.

'He has witnesses. A woman servant of mixed Spanish and Indian blood, called Rosina Perez, and her brother, Francisco, who is now employed in Sir Emmet's household.'

'Witnesses!' She was greatly surprised to learn that Sir Emmet, who had rather despised the Indians, had brought the brother and sister back to England with him. 'I assure you, they are lying as far as my own case is concerned. Whether or not Mr. Laurence was responsible for Lady Harley's death, I cannot be sure, but he always strongly denied it.'

Before the coach reached Callao, the Viceroy's soldiers had, to an extent, recovered from the surprise attack by a mixed crowd of up-country revolutionaries and men from *The Eagle*. The revolutionaries were neither sufficiently organised nor well-equipped to fight for long once their advantage was over, and soon fled into the countryside as a disordered rabble. The seamen from the pirate vessel were a more disciplined band, and as they retreated towards Callao, they methodically set fire to chosen buildings in order to divert their pursuers.

The Eagle, dark-painted and sleekly-lined, lay some hundred yards out on the roadstead, while her boats, oarsmen at the ready, were waiting as the coach jolted along the quay.

'No!'

Anne made one last effort to escape, but as she struggled against being removed from the coach, a soldier, ahead of his fellows, galloped towards the coach, pistol raised. It was hard to tell who fired first, but as the soldier fell from the impact of Captain Ducaine's ball, his own hit Robert Laurence who was trying to loosen Anne's grip on the door-frame of the coach. The shock of it as he reeled forward, wounded in the back, caused her to let go and fall too.

Christie began screaming, but the two girls were seized and bundled down steps into a waiting boat, whilst behind them, flames and smoke billowed up and out from the warehouses near the quay.

The next hours were ones of overwhelming fear, as she and Christie Waters, flung into a dark, hutchlike structure on the deck of *The Eagle*, clung desperately to each other as the ship tossed its way out into the great wastes of the Pacific Ocean.

It was night before the door was flung open and the glare of a lantern blazed into their weakened eyes. It was some moments before either could see properly, but then they distinguished the man as the mulatto who had driven the coach, his silver earrings reflecting the light as he gestured that they follow him.

'No. Your captain must come to see us!' Anne felt that she must try to retain some dignity, some slight edge over her captors, but Christie's words cut through her own.

'Let's get out of this place, Miss Anne!

It's so wet and smelly.'

The mulatto said nothing, but he gestured again, making a sign across his mouth conveying the message that he was mute and unable to talk. Lurching to the motion of the ship, the captives went before him down a narrow companionway.

The cabin into which they were ushered was low-ceilinged, but fitted out with fair comfort. Captain Ducaine sat behind a table which was rivetted to the decking, and he arose at their entry, even deigning a sort of half-bow.

'Pray be seated, ladies,' he said, and indicated a narrow bench.

'I shall stand,' retorted Anne, having, in spite of her fine words, to support herself with a hand against the bulkhead.

'That is unkind of you, ma'am. As you can see, it places me in danger of bumping my head.'

She then became aware that someone lay in the bunk, moaning intermittently. It was Robert Laurence, and impulsively, she went to him. He was conscious, but very pale and sweating heavily.

'He needs a surgeon!' she declared, forgetting her dislike of the planter, but seeing him only as a dangerously ill man.

'There is no surgeon on this ship,' said

66

Captain Ducaine, as if the matter were of no importance. 'The mate has removed the ball. If infection doesn't set in, Monsieur Laurent may survive.' He pronounced the surname in the French manner.

'He needs careful nursing. Anyone can see that. And why, sir, do you call him Monsieur?'

Ducaine laughed, and seated himself.

'I'm not going to stand any longer,' he announced. 'You may nurse the gentleman if you so wish. As for calling him Monsier — well, that's what he is. Monsieur Laurent of Martinique. I dare say you'll call him a spy and a traitor, but he's a loyal subject of both France and the Emperor.'

'Oh, God in heaven, save us both,' breathed Christie, hand to mouth in startlement. 'You're a Frenchie, too.'

'No, ma'am. I'm from Maine in the United States of America, although my great-great-grandfather came from Maine in France. Our name has become Ducaine, because that's how the backwoodsmen pronounced it.'

'And you're working for the French, too?'

Once again, he laughed. Captain Ducaine was a man who laughed frequently, but his eyes did not twinkle to match, remaining cold, a hunter's eyes, watching the every movement of his prey whilst using mirth as a diversionary tactic.

'I'm a privateer, ma'am. I work for whom I choose.'

He was not an ill-educated man, and certainly had not been roughly raised, but of all the men Anne had encountered during the short years of her life, he frightened her the most. Christie stared at him as if unable to remove her gaze; certainly, this sinister giant was someone quite outside her own experience.

'Then you'll do us the courtesy of explaining your plans for us.'

Once again, Anne was surprised at how clipped and self-assured her voice sounded. Inside, she was weak with fear and the dread that she and rosy-cheeked Christie were intended as playthings for his crew of assorted villains.

'I thought that I had made that clear, ma'am. I am keeping you as insurance. If we are unfortunate enough to encounter a British man-o'-war — unlikely in these waters — we may have to barter you to save our skins.'

'And until then?'

'I have had the ship's carpenter make some alterations in the cabin next to this one. I insist that you do not leave those quarters without my consent. Believe me, ladies, I wish you no ill, but I can't guarantee the behaviour of some of my men.'

As he said this, emphasising the word 'ladies', he smiled at Christie.

With her only weapon her pride, Anne realised that it was useless to fight.

'All right,' she said. 'But I would like to care for Mr. Laurence.' She deliverately used the English word Mister. 'I can hardly do so if he is in your cabin.'

Ducaine inclined his head slightly.

'I think you will have plenty of chances to come into this cabin while I'm absent,' he said. 'I'm master of this ship, ma'am, and spend the greatest part of my time seeing to her welfare.'

The new quarters allotted to the unwilling passengers were more acceptable than the crude prison in which they had been confined, and although much comfort was lacking, Anne knew that they could expect little else. At least, the cabin was adjacent to that of the captain, and although she both feared and detested him, she had to come to terms with the fact that he would protect them both for as long as it suited him.

'I wouldn't nurse that Monster Laurence,' said Christie, bitterly. 'I wouldn't do anything for any Froggie, and you know that, Miss Anne.'

Anne knew about the young husband who had died at Trafalgar, and she nodded sympathetically, but when she replied, she lowered her voice so that no would-be eavesdropper could hear.

'Listen,' she said, 'at least we should try to find out where we are going, and Mr. Laurence may tell us. Who knows, we may have a chance to escape.'

Christie groaned.

'But how, Miss Anne? We're out in the middle of the sea. We could be bound for China, for all we know.'

'I doubt it. If Captain Ducaine and Mr. Laurence stole the Apostles to help Bonaparte, we'll most likely sail north to the Isthmus, and if Mr. Laurence is from Martinique, it is likely he has plans for a new rising in the West Indies.'

Christie's expression became blank. Her sketchy geography did not permit her to grasp Anne's theory readily. In the morning, however, she showed that she had given this explanation some thought. They were, she declared, sailing west, for the sun was behind them.

The cabin was tiny and stifling, with minimal free space, for an extra bunk had been hastily constructed by the carpenter, and for hours, Anne had lain awake in the restlessness of exhaustion, longing for a free flow of air. Every time she closed her eyes, she saw again Inez lying dead, her lovely gown stained at the breast, and a dishevelled Robert Laurence grasping a pistol in his hand. Yet, sleep did come, solid and undreaming, so that it was Christie shaking her by the shoulder which roused her.

'Going west?' she repeated in a dazed voice, and then, in her mind's eye, she saw Emmet's big globe in his study at Whitestairs in England, and that large proportion of the earth's surface covered by the Pacific Ocean, dotted here and there by those specks of land discovered by the great mariners during the latter years of the previous century.

For the first time since her ordeal had begun on the previous morning, Anne began to weep. But tears were soon spent as the more mundane problems of their predicament asserted themselves. Not the least of these problems was that neither she nor Christie had a stitch beyond that which they were wearing. Her own gown, of a light satin striped fabric, was far too elaborate for the hard conditions in which she now found herself. Christie was a little better served in her practical cotton print, but both required a change of underclothing as well as outer garments.

'Perhaps there's something in the cargo that'll do,' said Christie hopefully.

'Perhaps. But I refuse to talk to Captain Ducaine about such a delicate matter,' replied Anne.

Still, a wash and a reasonably good breakfast refreshed her, and the weather remained steady so that the ship, while making good progress, did not rock and toss too disastrously. Thus, when the cabin boy told them that they could go on deck if they wished, captain's compliments, she felt a little more able to cope with the situation. The two girls had already decided to remain together at all times as a safety measure, and now they made their way cautiously up to the open air.

The ship was well run. There was none of the squalor and sloppiness which one might have expected to be part of what was, after all, a pirate vessel. An American flag fluttered cheekily at the stern, and to any casual observer, *The Eagle* was another of those well-built ships from the New England ports, heading out into the South Seas in search of trade, unfettered by any of the restrictive laws which still bound so many British merchantmen.

In the bright light of another tropical day, the corsairs who had raided and robbed Lima of the precious Apostles were fairly typical of any ship's crew of that time. Hard-bitten men of several nationalities, hoarsevoiced through the constant shouting required for working as a team aloft, they were now busy with the myriad jobs required to keep a ship in good sailing order.

After half an hour or so of taking the air in the small area of deck which had been set aside for them, Anne felt assured that Captain Ducaine would be about his duties for some time. Therefore, they both went below again, this time to the captain's cabin.

Robert Laurence still looked much as he had on the previous night. The mulatto, whom Anne now believed to be a personal servant to Ducaine, had been bathing the injured man's forehead, but when the two women entered, he made signs to show that they could take charge, and left.

'Ha, Miss Stacey, Ducaine said that you would come to nurse me!'

As he spoke, he managed a smile of sorts, and although he was directly responsible for the predicament in which she found herself, Anne smiled back. He was obviously in great pain, but bearing it so bravely that it was hard to be anything but sympathetic.

She had had little practical experience in

nursing, and it was Christie who knew what to do. Between them, they managed to make him more comfortable by lifting him into the half-sitting position he requested. He was very thirsty, but not hungry, having earlier refused breakfast.

'Don't force him,' whispered Christie. 'He'll eat when he's ready for it.'

Anne had to hold a cup to his lips. His hands had no strength and fell limply to the covers as he tried to help himself. After a while, he spoke.

'It was not my idea that you should be taken captive,' he said, in an exhausted voice.

'Do you know where we are going?' Anne asked.

'Ah! You'd best ask Captain Ducaine. I had made plans, but he had some of his own.' Then: 'You think me the lowest of traitors, Miss Stacey?'

'We are relying on whatever decent instincts you have to help us.'

He uttered a little croak of a laugh.

'So you are still the proud English lady? Now, listen. I, too, have been betrayed. I knew Ducaine some years ago in the West Indies, and in those days, he was an ordinary trader. When I left Lima before Christmas, I'd no notion that I would meet him again. I'd known immediately when I heard of the Apostles that they should be used to overthrow the regime in Peru, so I sought out a certain revolutionary leader and together we planned to capture the Apostles. We meant to melt them down to pay our forces so that we could gain control of the Viceroyalty of Peru and thus take away its support from the junta in Spain. By chance, *The Eagle* had come into this small port, and like a fool, I trusted Ducaine. Oh, he's for the Emperor as I am, but for his own gain. I did not know when I met Ducaine, by a trick of fate, that he had already raided several towns in New Spain, but with little success. Imagine my feelings, Miss Stacey, now that I know he always intended to betray my friends, and instead of taking the Apostles north as planned, is off across the Pacific, God only knows whither.'

He was very tired, but he had not finished talking. He had been speaking so quietly that Anne was leaning over him to catch every word. Christie, bored, was peering out of the porthole.

'It must be hard for you to understand why I set out to do what I could to foster revolution in a foreign country. Mine is the choice faced by many in my position. A father from one nation, a mother from another. Which to serve? The dying old order, or the bold new one?'

'Bonaparte is a monster. So many men have died because of him.'

'Ah, that is the price.'

His voice trailed away, and he fell asleep. Making sure that he was comfortable, Anne signalled Christie that they should leave. She had no desire to be confronted by Captain Ducaine here in his own quarters.

'What was he talking about?' asked Christie, curiously.

It was on the tip of Anne's tongue to tell the other, and then instinct made her prevaricate.

'He was a little delirious,' she said, firmly.

7

All that could be hoped was that Captain Ducaine would stick to his promise and shield both Anne and Christie from harm. Within a short time, it became obvious to Anne that to depend upon this hope would be both foolish and dangerous.

The captain, on the surface, was a surprisingly calm and affable man, but under this pose was a violent and murderous temper. About a week out of Callao, as *The Eagle* moved across the endlessly huge ocean, the only object of human origin betwixt sea and sky, with the occasional seabird or the surfacing of some aquatic creature to break the sheer vast isolation, a seaman, whether through deafness or design, did not leap to his captain's command.

At Ducaine's orders, he was seized, lashed to a mast and flogged by the mulatto, Daniel. Anne, who had been taking her daily turn at walking back and forth across the tiny scrap of deck allotted to the female prisoners for the purpose of exercise, watched horrified before running away, and hastening down to the cabin. The difficulties arising from their lack of spare clothing meant that Christie was below at the time, waiting for some of her garments to dry.

'We'd best keep on his good side, then,' said Christie drily, as Anne described the reason for the cries and moans which reached them.

'How can you talk like that!'

'I want to stay alive,' retorted Christie, and then she looked slyly at her mistress, hazel eyes speculative in her rosy-cheeked face. 'I'm goin' to ask him whether there's anything on the ship we could wear.'

'No! We mustn't ask favours. Once we do . . . ' Anne's voice trailed away helplessly.

'I'm going to.'

'I forbid it.'

Christie had the strangest expression on her face, as if she were undergoing a transformation.

'We're not mistress and maid now,' she said. Christie had a slow, country way of speaking, but her meaning was concise enough. She saw the reality. They were both in this predicament, and on an equal footing.

'The captain's looked at me a bit particular,' she continued. 'There's no need for things to be worse 'n they are.'

'Christie Waters! Captain Ducaine is a

common pirate, and an enemy of our country. If he's caught, he'll be hanged from the nearest yardarm.

'He's a Yankee. If he wants to work for the Frenchies, he can.'

Exasperated, Anne raised her hand to slap Christie, but then realised how futile such an act would be. She was as startled as the French aristocrats who, two decades before, had discovered that the servants they had always taken for granted were human beings with feelings and ideas of their own.

'I'd expected more loyalty from you,' said Anne, angrily.

Christie's gaze held her steadily for some seconds before she replied.

'I've a right to live,' she said, in a low, fierce whisper. 'And if I can, I shall.'

Thus Christie determined her own path, and yet there was more to it than a mere urge for survival. The young woman, who, since her widowhood, had been standoffish to any overtures, had been stirred into a new awakening of desire by the surface pleasantness and carelessly concealed savagery of Captain Ducaine.

Neither was he unaffected by the admiring glances and small smiles she tossed in his direction. Bolts of cloth were brought up from the hold, gay lengths of brightly printed calico meant for trade in the South Seas.

Robert Laurence was now well enough to come up on deck, and he sat under the awning which provided a little shade for the two female prisoners when their cabin was too stifling. He was still weak, and his recovery was painfully slow. Normally a vigorous young man, he was finding his convalescence extremely boring. As well, he was plainly worried by the turn events had taken.

However, he found it hard to hide his amusement as Anne turned away in disgust from the stuffs which Christie examined and assessed, while Captain Ducaine, smiling slightly, watched from one side.

'This one, and this,' said Christie, quite imperiously, to the mulatto, who then turned to his master for explanation.

The captain made a few swift signs with his fingers, and the mulatto obediently placed two of the bolts to one side. A seaman staggered away under the weight of the remainder.

'And which will which lady wear?' asked Ducaine, looking insolently towards Anne, who was trying to ignore the whole charade.

There was a sure and certain way to Christie's heart, she thought, contemptuously, and that was the way in which Ducaine repeatedly referred to the servant as a lady. It had quite turned the silly creature's head.

'The blue for Miss Stacey and the yellow for Christie,' drawled Robert Lawrence, and the way in which he differentiated between the two did not go unnoticed by Christie, who tossed her dark locks and sent the planter a venomous look.

Captain Ducaine laughed and said that he had to return to his duties, but as he turned, he reached out and touched Christie's arm, a mere brush of the fingers, but a gesture which told the girl that in his eyes there was no difference between her and her mistress.

Anne sat down alongside Laurence. With the coldness which had arisen between her and Christie, she needed to talk to someone, and she had to admire, grudgingly, the fortitude with which the Creole had borne his injury.

'The mulatto gives me the shivers,' she said quietly, as Christie gathered up her lengths of cloth and went below. It was extremely hot, with a falling wind causing the ship's canvas to hang limply, and *The Eagle*'s progress westward had now slowed to a sluggish and heaving crawl through the wavelets, in many ways harder for the squeamish to bear than the livelier movement of a brisk wind pushing the ship forward.

'Daniel? Oh, he's harmless enough, and the only man on board Ducaine can really trust. He depends on his master, you see, to act as his ears and mouth. And unlike other serfs, he cannot free himself from that bondage.'

She knew that he was referring to Christie, and she bit her lips angrily.

'My family rescued her from a foundling home. And after she had left us to marry, we took her back again when she lost her husband at Trafalgar. She was quite destitute, and begged to return.'

'Ah,' said Robert Laurence. 'She has a fine instinct for self-preservation, perhaps? Or has she simply found a chance for freedom?'

In spite of everything, she began to feel a liking of sorts for Robert Laurence. He had a certain cynical common sense which saved her from wallowing in self pity.

'In theory,' he persisted, 'the English common man is free. In fact, he is as much a serf as a tied peasant in France before 1789.'

'You're a fine one to talk of freedom,' she flashed back. 'You are a slave-owner, are you not? There are Englishmen who've devoted their lives to end the dreadful slave trade.'

'But they don't see the slaves all about them! There is something romantic about a black African being snatched from his jungle, isn't there? And a feeling of self-satisfaction because one is noble enough to care? Those fine Englishmen worry because the man who picks the cotton is black, but what of the poor wretch who spins the cotton in a vile and steamy factory?'

'My own father worked hard to help bring about the end of the slave trade,' she retorted. 'He was aware that there are evils in his own country, Mr. Laurence, but the worst evil had to be destroyed first.'

Laurence laughed, and she flushed, annoyed because she had allowed herself to be drawn into an argument with him, thus providing him with amusement.

'I can see that you are growing into one of those formidable Englishwomen,' he teased, but unexpectedly, his mood changed, and his tone became grave and urgent.

'There are more important things for us to discuss,' he said, quietly. 'I beg you, Miss Stacey, to show some amiability towards Peter Ducaine. Our lives are in his hands. I owe him a debt for not leaving me to be captured back there in Callao, but he has betrayed me once. And another thing, Miss Stacey, I know that always you think of me as a murderer. Oh, a sick murderer, who deserved your Christian pity but you are wrong.'

His eyes, under their deeply arched brows, met hers steadily, willing her to believe him.

'Lady Harley was leaving an intolerable marriage to start a new life with me. I thought that her husband did not suspect. I even flirted a little with you, Miss Stacey, to deceive him, which annoyed Inez very much. But he killed Inez. Of that I am sure.'

He was putting into words her own agonised thoughts of many a tossing night in her bunk.

'Consider, Miss Stacey. I was leaving Lima that day. Why should I have killed Inez? No, Sir Emmet was the guilty one. He discovered that she was eloping, followed her, and in the quarrel, shot her.'

'My guardian is not a man of passionate feelings,' she answered, but the doubt was there. Outwardly, Sir Emmet was so controlled, so sure of his role as a manipulator, that one could only guess at his real feelings.

'I loved Inez,' concluded Robert Laurence, simply. 'I would not have harmed her.'

Before she could think of something to say in reply, their attention was mutually taken by the reappearance of Christie Waters from down below. She was resolute, and walked with her easy stride, unhampered now by the movement of the ship, for the sea had become quite calm as the last vestige of wind failed. *The Eagle* no longer moved at all, and the sunlight shimmered down on water glassily green except for patches of seaweed lying darkly beneath the surface.

Christie's simple cotton dress had faded from frequent washing in seawater, and it had tightened across the bust, showing up her somewhat statuesque lines boldly. Without hesitation, she walked to the bridge, where Captain Ducaine stood with his mate, an Irishman happy to be involved in a venture against the Anglo-Saxon. The Yankee scanned the distance through his glass, alert for the dark streaking of cloud or a line of breakers which might indicate a rising wind. As Christie passed, a common sailor, on all fours as he scrubbed a patch of deck, looked up appreciatively, his creased and sunburnt face reflecting the desire stirred by this young and voluptuous woman.

'Trouble,' muttered Robert Laurence. 'Doesn't she realise . . . ?'

Christie went straight to the captain. She wanted some needles and thread. Cloth was all very well, but she needed more to stitch some sort of covering for her decency.

Neither Anne nor the Creole heard what the captain said, but Christie returned with a flaunting of anger, her cheeks red from more than heat, followed by the eyes of a dozen seamen already bored by the tedium of being becalmed.

'I want you,' said Robert Laurence quietly, 'to be very careful and watchful. Remember, Miss Stacey, taking you hostage was none of my doing, but in my present weak state, I can do very little to help you. Sitting here, I've had time to observe, and to listen. There are men on this ship, Miss Stacey, who will do anything on God's earth to possess the Apostles, and as well, they covert both yourself and your servant.'

8

Later that day, the mulatto came to Anne with a tray bearing threads, needles and scissors, taken from the supply of trade goods on board. She gave them to Christie, who was still sulking in the cabin. Feeling that she had an advantage following the other's rebuff by the captain, she told Christie of Robert Laurence's warning. Christie considered this for a few moments. Then:

'Where are these idols?' she demanded. 'You'd 'a' thought they'd have a guard over them. But there's none. If they're in the hold with the cargo, anyone could take them, if they had a mind to.'

'I think they're in the captain's cabin,' said Anne.

'There's no one here half the day,' pointed out Christie. 'Not now that Mr. Laurence is up and about.' She began fanning herself. 'It's so hot. Oh, Miss Anne, I do wish we were safe home in England. Where are we going?'

The Eagle was becalmed for eight days. Once a breeze did spring up, and the listless men leapt to the commands of their officers to take advantage of the zephyr, but within the hour, the sails had slackened and *The Eagle* once more rocked idly on the barely perceptible swell.

To take their minds off these difficult conditions, Anne and Christie joined efforts in their first attempt at dressmaking. Together, they used their own garments as patterns, and Anne sat patiently over long seams, using stitches half-forgotten from her nursery sampler days. The results, two long shifts with little shape or style, would have earned nothing but contempt from a regular seamstress, but they provided a welcome change.

'At least it is cooler than my poor gown,' admitted Anne, donning her new attire. Clumsy the garment may have been, but she had a pleasing feeling of accomplishment.

In a way, she was sorry they had finished their sewing for the time being. The task had kept Christie occupied, and her mind off the way in which Ducaine had snubbed her. Since then, she had treated the captain coolly, and for Anne this was the greatest relief. It was some time before Christie told her what the buccaneer had said.

'He said I shouldn't walk so boldly.'

Ducaine, Anne thought silently, had been within his rights to say that, but she passed no comment, remembering with uneasiness what Laurence had said to her at the time. His hints at mutiny had frightened her, but since then, the ship's company had seemed contented enough, passing spare time fishing, practising swordplay, or shooting at bottles tossed overboard.

On the other hand, lying on her bunk the previous night, Anne had heard from the next cabin some angry words pass between Ducaine and the partner in conspiracy whom he had betrayed.

'You're crazy!' Laurence had said. 'We'd have served France better by helping Felipe Ramerez back in Peru.'

'If my scheme works, the Emperor will have all he has ever desired, and I, my friend, shall be the equal of princes.'

I wonder, thought Anne, when the voices had faded away, why Ducaine bothered to save Robert Laurence. She decided to sound out the planter at the first opportunity.

This came when she went up on deck wearing her new shift.

'Now that you are so clever, you must mend my other shirt,' stated Laurence, who was sitting in his usual spot under the awning.

Looking at him, she could see that the heat was affecting him, which was all the more worrying as he had spent all his life in the tropics. It was as if he had recovered only to a degree, and must stay a partial invalid for the rest of his days.

'I'll fan you for a while,' she offered, genuinely disturbed by his pallor. Clutching coldly at her heart was the terror of knowing that, whether or not he had murdered Inez in a fit of passion, he was still her only real ally on board, for she suspected that Captain Ducaine had only to exert his charm and Christie would be under his spell again.

'Ah, thank you. That would be good.'

As he spoke, he lifted his right hand, and looked at it, as if bemused.

'I've always been so strong, and I thought that I was mending,' he admitted. 'But inside, Miss Stacey, there is something which will not heal. At first, when I was so ill, I wished to die, to join poor Inez, but after all, life is still sweet.' Then, broodingly, he added, 'Perhaps it would have been best if I had died on Callao quay. I'm not a man to lie about half helpless.'

'If you had died, I should be in the vilest straits,' she whispered, and then, noticing that no one was within earshot, she continued, all the while fanning. 'Why did the captain save you if he had betrayed your friends?'

His mouth twisted cynically.

'He needs me. His heart is French, but his language is Yankee English. He cannot speak French.' Then he laughed. 'You are trying to wheedle Ducaine's plans out of me, eh? No, I shall not tell you.'

'I thought that you would help me,' she reproached him, almost in tears.

'But I shall. Trust me. If we don't die of thirst and heat in this wretched place, we shall be making landfall at Tahiti once the wind rises,' he promised. 'The island is an independent kingdom with its own ruler, but I believe that there is some traffic between Tahiti and Sydney in New South Wales, which is British.'

She recollected that the Westons, the missionaries who had offered to escort her back to England, had come from Tahiti. Oh, please God, she prayed, let there still be some other English people on the island.

'I'll do everything I can,' he added. 'But don't say a word to that woman Christie. I don't trust her.'

The night settled down, airless and silent, with only the slight lapping of the water about the ship to break the vast silence of that empty stretch of the Pacific. Christie came in late, humming to herself.

'I've been talking to the captain,' she said.

'He's been pointing out the different stars to me.'

Robert Laurence is right, thought Anne wearily. She is not to be trusted. That man Ducaine has merely to crook his little finger in her direction, and she goes running.

'I wish we could leave the door open,' continued Christie. 'It's like an oven down here. Captain says the glass is falling.'

'You've been talking a great amount with the captain,' snapped Anne. 'Remember, if we are saved, it will do you no good to have been so friendly with a common pirate.'

'He has cause,' flashed back Christie. 'His uncle was killed in the War of Independence, and his brother was pressganged into the British navy, and him a Yankee on a Yankee ship. Captain Ducaine has never heard from him since.'

'Seeing that Captain Ducaine is roaming the seas, that isn't surprising,' said Anne, acidly.

Christie, undressed, flopped down on her bunk. Anne turned over on her side to attempt to find sleep, but at that moment, she was stirred by a sound, an increasing mutter of voices and then shouting and the thud of feet across the deck. Three shots startled her into sitting up, hand to her throat.

'Come on out, Cap'n. We've taken the ship!'

The two girls were both out of their narrow bunks in a second, feeling about for their clothes, pulling their gaudy, shapeless cotton gowns over their heads, dressing as an instinctive protection.

'Don't be fools!'

The voice with an Irish accent belonged to the mate, and his reply was a volley of abuse. There was another shot, and yells.

'Oh, God preserve us!' Christie forgot her pertness and new-found independence and drew close to Anne in the darkness.

There was some parleying with Ducaine, who was apparently in some sort of protective shelter.

'We wants those idols!'

'Find them yourself.'

All this was accompanied by shouting and yelling somewhere in the distance, muffled as if by walls. For the girls, in the dark and stuffy cabin, minutes passed in increasing terror, climaxed as fists pounded on the door. They both kept silent, hoping frantically that the mutineers would believe the cabin to be empty, but then timbers crashed and split as an axe smashed in the barrier.

The struggling women were forced up the companionway, and on to the deck where they were hauled forward to stand under the one lantern which illuminated the excited faces of the mutineers. Anne realised that Ducaine was in the small deckhouse which had been their prison when they had first been brought aboard *The Eagle*. He was obviously armed, which was why he had not been overcome.

Stepping forward, the ringleader, who was that same seaman who had more than once cast lecherous glances at Christie, brandished his knife under Anne's chin, missing the flesh by the mere fraction of an inch. She willed herself to stay still, determined not to show this human carrion that his action almost made her heart stop from sheer terror.

'Now Cap'n,' jeered this man, who, for obvious reasons, was known by his fellows as Two-fingered Ned, 'what's it to be? The wimmen, or them golden idols?'

Beneath the planking of the deck, there was shouting and thumping. Imprisoned down below, there were other men, those who had not joined the mutineers.

'Look 'ere!'

Anne was dragged some paces forward, and her face held forcefully so that she had to look upwards, whilst one of the men held the lantern aloft. The mate hung limply from a spar, a knotted rope about his neck.

'Now you tell the cap'n what's goin' to 'appen to ye, me fine gentry mort. After we's 'ad our bit o' fun with ye.'

'Let me go, you filthy creature!' Her voice came out low and intense, and Two-fingered Ned roared with laughter.

'So there's a bit o' life under those proud airs. Who'd a thought it to see you strut about like a crow in a gutter!'

'Never mind 'er. Let's find the idols first,' cried one of the other mutineers.

'Don't be fools out there. The glass is falling. We'll keel over if you don't look sharp and get about your work,' shouted Ducaine.

A roar of derisive laughter greeted his words, and Christie was shoved towards the deckhouse, kicking and struggling.

'Here's yer dell, Cap'n. Come on, mort, tell 'im what's going to 'appen to ye if he don't give us the idols.'

Sheet lightning flared across the sky, illuminating the whole scene, the dishevelled and drunken crew members, one with a bloody bandage about his arm, and another, dead or unconscious, in the scuppers. This flash also gave the truth about the numbers of the mutineers, a mere eight all told, which meant that the greater part of the crew was below, thumping and shouting for release all the more energetically as the first thunder of the tropical storm boomed and rolled all about them.

Two-fingered Ned ignored the approaching fury, and, whilst one of his companions held Christie's arm behind her back, thrust his crippled left hand down the neck of her gown. She cried out, and the door of the deckhouse was flung open.

Ducaine held a pistol in one hand and a belaying pin in the other. Behind him was the mulatto, knife in hand. Lightning rampaged across the sky in great sheets as the mutineers circled the two like wild dogs. Anne ran to a hatch and began struggling with the fastenings as the ship lurched under the first blast of the hurricane. Two-fingered Ned clasped her about the waist and pulled her back against him, whilst Christie was similarly held by another mutineer.

'Go on, cap'n,' he yelled. 'Shoot!'

The truth dawned on Anne, the real reason why Ducaine, the ruthless and apparently fearless, had taken refuge in the deckhouse. The one charge in his pistol had accounted for the mutineer who lay motionless, and for the past minutes he had been attempting to bluff his opponents into believing that he was able to hold them at bay. Now his bluff had been called. With a curse, he flung his pistol to the deck.

'All right,' he said. 'Let the women go free. I'll give you the damned gold.'

Anne felt Two-fingered Ned's grip loosen: at the same time, he uttered a kind of gurgle, and fell limply to the deck, and as the ship heaved, slid into the darkness beyond the lantern's rays. Then the reason for Ducaine's meek surrender was revealed.

'Catch!' cried Robert Laurence, and in one graceful movement he had snatched up Ned's pistol and tossed it across to Ducaine, who caught it with one hand whilst bracing himself with the other. Laurence himself held a sword, stained with Ned's blood, for his quick and skilful thrust had killed the mutineer instantly.

Suddenly, the tables were turned. Without their leader, the rebels were dispirited, and as a man, bolted forward, while *The Eagle* reeled before the increasing force of the gale.

It was a long and terrible night, with Ducaine himself lashed to the helm as he fought the storm with every ounce of strength and skill in his powerful body. Seas swamped the deck repeatedly, pouring down into the captain's cabin, where Christie, half-sobbing, but somehow clinging to her courage, tried to help Anne as the latter did all she could for Robert Laurence.

The mutineers had either overlooked him, believing the Creole to be an invalid, or had considered him to be of no account. Instead, Laurence had overset their plans, and saved all the others. There could never be any doubt of that. In so doing, he had sacrificed his own life, for his efforts had opened the barely healed internal wound which had kept him in such a weakened state. When she realised that he was dying, Anne wept openly.

He was a spy, and a traitor to the English who had trusted him, but he was also a man of daring who had risked much for the cause in which he believed.

It was obvious that he was sinking fast and aware of it, for he muttered a prayer in French as Anne leaned over and begged him to tell her the truth about Lady Harley's death.

Had he killed Inez?

'No, I did not kill her.' Then he looked past her, eyes glazing. 'Inez. Ma cherie. Ma vie.'

He died, quite peacefully, as the worst of the storm spent itself.

His passing did not make any difference to the actual handling of the ship, for he had been a passenger, but four other men had perished during that night, for as well, Two-fingered Ned's chief confederate had gone overboard.

'It saves me having to deal with him,' drawled Ducaine, but there was an iciness in his eyes which told Anne the truth.

Who would query a man overboard during such a violent storm? This quick solution saved the captain the risk of arousing more ill feeling, for he was now short-handed and needed every man.

There was another direct result of the mutiny which had led to Robert Laurence's death. Anne now occupied the passenger's cabin alone, for Christie had moved into the captain's quarters, taking over the space once used by the Creole.

9

With the death of Robert Laurence, who, in his own way, had been her friend, and Christie openly established as Ducaine's mistress, Anne pinned her hopes on finding a chance to escape at Tahiti. She convinced herself that this would be possible, because, not only would *The Eagle* be taking on supplies of fresh food, but Captain Ducaine hoped to sign on extra hands willing to undertake the rest of his mysterious and dangerous voyage.

As he had told her, Robert Laurence had been aware of their ultimate destination, but Anne was sure that now no one but the captain himself knew. Even Christie, sharing his bed, had not yet been able to wheedle that out of him, but, quite infatuated and overwhelmed by the Yankee's forceful character, she was happy to place her fate in his hands.

'He's told me that I'm going to be as good as a princess,' she said to Anne, with that irritating little toss of the head and raising of the nose which comes so easily to some women of no particular background when they think that wealth and position are to be theirs. Whilst not actually ordering her former mistress about, she was often very patronising in her manner.

What rubbish, thought Anne, and became all the more determined to escape at Tahiti.

'Land ahoy!'

The lookout's cry aroused them all. Nothing but a faint shadow on the horizon was yet visible, but in another hour, a dark green mountain rose out of the sea. It was a small island, relic of some primeval upheaval which had thrust this peak up from the ocean floor. To eyes starved of land for weeks, it was incredibly beautiful, clothed with luxuriant foliage which grew right to the water's edge, whilst white seabirds flew in vast flocks about its summit.

They saw more islands that day, each seemingly a little larger and more beautiful than the last. Anne stood for hours at the rail as *The Eagle* skimmed along with a fair breeze behind, forgetting all the horror as each new vista of loveliness spread out before her. Zigzagging mountain ranges reared up from exquisite lagoons edged by thatched huts built no more than a few yards back from the sandy beaches. Everywhere there were the outrigger canoes of the natives, tiny shells meant for fishing within the confines of the lagoons, and the larger, heavier craft which travelled from one island to another, for these were a seafaring people. In absolute contrast to the peaceful lagoons were coasts which rose sheer out of the sea, glistening with waterfalls which cascaded down between trees and bushes growing horizontally out from what appeared to be solid rock.

These were the enchanted islands which had been introduced to the world by the writings of Captain Cook and his botanist passenger, Joseph Banks. Cook had not discovered Tahiti (or Otaheite as some called it), but it was his voyage thither to observe the transit of Venus which had given Europe its first real glimpses of the pagan, sensual, and yet strangely innocent world of Polynesia. Despite her troubles, Anne felt a thrill of anticipation at the chance of seeing fabled Tahiti, with its beautiful women and exotic customs.

The Westons had worked on Tahiti as missionaries, and had failed. Mrs. Weston had spoken of the natives as being children of darkness, but while suppressing her abiding disgust for many of their customs, she had admitted that the Tahitians had a certain charm, although evils introduced by looseliving Europeans had aggravated their wicked ways.

It was back in 1796 that the Westons had set out for Tahiti as members of a thirty-strong band determined to win the natives for Christianity. Some of the pilgrims had been murdered, others had been driven out by Polynesians who strongly resisted attempts at conversion, and the Westons had simply ceased trying. Anne hoped that some of the party still remained, and that she could beg their assistance.

The Eagle's anchor was dropped in a large bay with an incredibly beautiful backdrop of mountains, and before the ship's sails were furled, dozens of canoes were skimming out from the beach. At this moment, Anne was roughly seized by Captain Ducaine, half dragged down the companionway, and thrust into her cabin.

'I know what's in your mind, Ma'am,' he mocked. 'But you're too precious to me to be allowed to escape.'

With that, the door was locked. In vain, she called out and beat her fists against the unyielding wood. Ducaine had forestalled her.

From her porthole, she saw the handsome natives of Tahiti, fleeting glimpses as they came close to the ship in their canoes, their young women calling out coquettishly to the seamen and the men eager to trade and steal.

Their discovery by Europeans was but a generation earlier, but already many of their native skills had been degraded. Gaudy cotton cloth was replacing the beautiful tapa (beaten mulberry bark) cloth which had clothed the Tahitians of Cook's day, but they were still a fine-looking people, from what Anne could see as they passed within her limited outlook from the porthole. Their complexions varied from a deep olive to brown, the women's hair was luxuriant and glossily black, and their features, although heavy and a little too strongboned for her fancy, were pleasing and handsome, but often marred by tattooing. Although vivacious and carefree, they were not impractical, and were eager to trade fruit and fish, and the curios they knew Europeans coveted.

The Polynesians had awakened quickly to the advantages of the souvenir trade. They made all sorts of oddments which seafarers could take home to decorate their cottages in their retirement. There were paddles which did not paddle, ladles which could not ladle, and weapons which would have splintered if put to the test, all decorated by a travesty of their traditional carvings. In return, they wanted iron, nails, small axes and fish hooks — and the muskets which would give them the advantage in tribal conflicts.

Her confinement in the cabin soon became intolerable. The days were warm and humid, and there were times when she felt that she was gasping for breath. The meals brought to her by the cabin boy were some compensation, with delicious fresh fruits, many of them strange to her, and vegetables, as well as fresh pork and fish.

Anne's longing for freedom grew almost into an obsession. She felt that she was going mad, and to try to keep herself from yielding to the misery which threatened to swallow up her whole mind and body, she forced herself to walk back and forth in the tiny space available. She tried all means to keep herself occupied. She counted up to a thousand. She repeated the variations of every French verb which came to mind. She carried on conversations with herself in her limited Spanish. And she sat down and thought through the circumstances of Inez's death.

On that morning, Inez had believed that she would be eloping with Robert Laurence to a new life, perhaps in the West Indies or New Spain. To allay suspicion, she had dressed as if attending the service at the cathedral, but had slipped away, unnoticed by anyone except her maid, Rosina. The Peruvian, in spite of Christie's dislike and allegations, was sufficiently loyal to the household to tell Anne what had occurred. Sir Emmet, during this time, was ostensibly in his study, with his secretary.

But was he ?

To the cold and calculating baronet, Inez had been merely a stepping stone for ambition. Would her attempted elopement have thrown him into such a passion that he would have shot her at point blank range?

Anne pondered over her second cousin's character. He had thwarted her marriage to Anthony Bretherton for the sole reason that the personable and well-to-do young man could not forward Emmet's own career. He was completely selfish, and yet with a curious and intense streak of patriotism. Was that the answer? Did he see poor Inez's flight after happiness as treachery to the British cause in South America?

What was the use of thinking about it now, Anne told herself, going to the porthole and peering out. It was unlikely that she would ever see Emmet, or Anthony, again. What would happen to her once her usefulness as a hostage was expended? Would she be marooned on an island somewhere in this vast Pacific?

This last was what she feared above all else, and hopelessness again descended on her. In complete contrast to her own misery, she could see almost naked fishermen pulling in their nets, laughing gaily and calling out to one another as they did so. Slim brown children played in the shallows, whilst their elder sisters took the day's catch in baskets back to their open-sided thatched houses, built amidst palms and flowering trees. It was a scene of idyllic happiness.

As she watched, she saw *The Eagle's* longboat being propelled towards the shore by strongly wielded oars. In the stern sat Captain Ducaine, wearing the straw hat decorated with ribbons which Anne recalled from their first meeting. At his side was Christie, her dark locks embellished by a wreath of multi-coloured flowers, a gift probably from the natives, who were so fond of decorating their own persons with the beautiful blooms which flourished in this moist tropical climate.

Much later, when a half-grown moon hung in the sky, Anne heard the chanting and saw the glow of many fires on shore. There was a native celebration of some kind in progress. She guessed that the ship was almost deserted, with most of the crew ashore at the entertainment, and she sought about anew for some means of escape. For a few insane moments she considered trying to force herself through the porthole, but if she did, could she clamber up to the deck, and if she fell, how long would she survive in the water? Swimming was not part of a young English lady's education. Alternatively, if she called out, perhaps someone would come, and she could hit him on the head and run from the cabin. But, what then? There was no purpose in escaping from the cabin if she could not leave the ship.

Anne sat down, fists clenched as she gave way to her anger and frustration in bitter tears. Courage had quite gone. She wanted to die, to escape forever from an existence of nightmare so far removed from the luxury of her former life that there were times when she doubted whether she really were Miss Anne Stacey, heiress and gentlewoman.

'Do not despair!'

Who had spoken? Had she imagined it? She thrust her face to the porthole, straining her eyes. Outside, the waters were silver and barely stirring beneath the moon. From whence had that voice come? Below her, there was a faint splashing, and then one of the light native canoes used within the lagoon skimmed away towards the beach. Above, on the deck, a sailor on watch called out hoarsely.

'Away with ye, ye thievin' savage!'

Anne was sure that the occupant of the canoe had not been a native intent on stealing whatever he could find. The voice had been English, a good voice, with a touch of the provinces about it. Someone outside the complement of *The Eagle* knew that she was a prisoner.

There was a little lift to her spirits, and she washed her face and brushed her hair, before peering out again trying to discern what was happening on that small piece of shore within her vision. The fires still glowed, but on the beach itself, there was nothing except the canoes drawn up and the nets hanging on their frames.

The Eagle remained at Tahiti for another two days, and on the second morning, as the crew busied themselves in preparation for setting sail, a canoe came to the ship's side, carrying two Europeans. Anne saw them for a moment. They were both young men, and roughly dressed in a mixture of ragged sailors' garb and tattered trade clothing.

She was released from the cabin almost as soon as the ship set sail from its anchorage, followed through the opening in the reef by dozens of Tahitian canoes, whose occupants cried out sad farewells and threw garlands after the departing vessel.

Captain Ducaine stood behind the helmsman, and he nodded briefly at her, barely taking his eyes from the ominous froth of white water beyond the reef. The sailors seemed more cheerful than formerly, although one or two waved back at the girls who cried out so sorrowfully after *The Eagle*.

'The wahines 'll have forgotten the fools by tomorrow,' said Ducaine, to no one in particular. 'That's their nature.'

Anne ignored him and walked to the rail, breathing in the fresh breeze, so glad to be out of her prison that for a little while she forgot the fear and hatred with which she regarded Captain Ducaine and all his crew. The island behind them was incredibly beautiful, and the afternoon sun bathed the high peaks. She was surprised at how many people were on the beaches, and at how many canoes were drawn up along the strand. Tahiti was an amazingly populous island, and it was equally astonishing that so small a piece of land could maintain so many people of a comparatively primitive culture. From the little she had seen of the natives, they appeared to be happy and well fed. She had, of course, no knowledge of the bloody internecine wars which periodically decimated the population, and like many transient visitors, saw only the benevolent face of Polynesia.

'I've seen harbours like this one thick with war canoes,' said Captain Ducaine, coming to her side, 'and their chiefs done up to glory in their wicker armour and feather helmets. They're the world's best sailors. I wanted to recruit a couple of them to make up my crew, but King Pomare wouldn't let them go.'

'When are you going to let *me* go,' she demanded, in a fierce whisper, 'Why are you keeping me on this ship? You could have put me ashore on the island. I can do you no harm. I don't know where you are going, or why.'

'Ma'am, you're my hostage and my insurance, and now that there's a married woman aboard, you've no need to fear for your reputation.'

As he spoke, the cold eyes mocked her, and she knew that he took pleasure in his power over her. She represented all that he hated, England and privileged birth.

'Do you mean that you've brought another woman on board?' she exclaimed.

Ducaine laughed in that strange, curiously mirthless way of his.

'No, ma'am,' he responded. 'Parson Nott,

back there on Tahiti, was good enough to bind me and Christie Waters in holy matrimony. It did the poor fellow the world of good to be able to perform his Christian rites. He gets little enough chance amongst those heathen, with King Pomare not able to make up his mind whether to kick him out or sacrifice him up to their own gods.'

'You've married Christie!' She could scarcely believe her ears.

'We took to one another from the first,' said Ducaine, carelessly. 'I'm a New Englander, Miss Stacey, and we're a proper lot at bottom.'

'Proper!'

She echoed the word and turned away. Christie had gone over to the enemy with a vengeance, and somehow, tying herself in marriage to this buccaneer seemed worse than being his mistress. At that instant, Christie herself came on to deck, very pleased with herself and her new status as captain's wife. Rather surprisingly, she came from the direction of the forecastle, and carried a bowl and a towel. Before she spoke, she flung the contents of the bowl over the side.

'The tall one's feeling well enough now,' she said to her husband, 'though the other's still poorly. You shouldn't 'a' allowed him to be hit so hard.'

'They both struggled too much,' retorted Ducaine, while members of the crew who were nearby smirked. 'You know as well as I do that we asked 'em nicely to join us.'

'You mean that you kidnapped them,' said Anne, bluntly.

Christie shook her head warningly at Anne, as if telling her not to aggravate Ducaine, but the captain walked away, apparently considering his other duties more pressing than chit-chat with women.

The Eagle had now hit the full swell of the open ocean, although other islands formed shadowy shapes all about as the sun sank to the horizon. With the movement, both Anne and Christie had to steady themselves against whatever support was to hand.

'They're English, same as you an' me,' said Christie, after a few awkward moments during which both young women assessed their altered position in life, 'Convicts who've escaped from Botany Bay. They came across on a Yankee whaler, but deserted. They were hoping to do some trading with us so they could get some proper shoes. Captain Ducaine asked them both, polite like, to join the ship's company, but they said they liked it better on the island with the wahines — that's what the young Tahitian women are called — so the captain had them taken prisoner. We need extra hands if we're to reach the Indies, after losing those men in the mutiny and then the storm.'

The Indies! This was the first intimation that Anne had heard of their ultimate destination. East or West? Robert Laurence had known, but he had refused to tell her. The East Indies were, of course, nominally part of the Dutch overseas empire, although now under French influence.

Once, she had asked Anthony Bretherton why it was so necessary for the French to be routed from Spain, for being in love, she naturally resented the war which would take him away from her again. There were two reasons, she was told. One was to protect the British right of access to the Mediterranean, where Boney had received such a pasting at the mouth of the Nile, and the other was to occupy as many French troops as possible, for Napoleon longed to conquer the East.

'Everything wears out,' Napoleon had said a full decade earlier, when he was still a triumphant and ambitious young general. 'My glory is already past: this tiny Europe does not offer enough of it. We must go to the East; all great glory has always been gained there.'

Admiral Nelson had made nonsense of that boast on the sea, and General Wellesley had destroyed French hopes in India.

What was it she had overheard Ducaine saying to poor Robert Laurence? If his plan succeeded, he would be the equal of princes!

Anne did not dare question Christie further. She had to hope for casually dropped hints, but she felt a brief excitement at once quelled by the hopelessness of her situation. She was almost sure that Captain Ducaine intended to use the Apostles to help the French in the East. The West Indies were now held too securely by the British to make even the wildest and most daring scheme practicable.

But . . . of what use was this knowledge, if it were correct?

She was a prisoner, out in the middle of the world's vastest ocean.

'Do not despair!'

The three words spoken in that good solid midlands English voice returned to her mind. That had been no dream. One did not dream such a voice, and the watch up on deck had seen and heard *someone*.

She must obey the command. She had been spared during the mutiny and in the terrible storm which had followed. There was a purpose to it. She had to believe that.

It was necessary to remain on friendly

terms with Christie, for she knew where they were bound, and why. Ducaine's mad schemes had fascinated the former servant probably as much as the man's forceful personality, and if Ducaine hoped to become the equal of princes, it must be heady stuff for Christie to have the chance of becoming a princess.

10

The next morning, Anne saw the two convicts who were the new and unwilling recruits to *The Eagle's* crew. The younger, little more than a boy, was short and stocky, with reddish hair cut rather jaggedly to the level of his earlobes, and a slightly pockmarked and very sunburnt complexion. He also had a bruise and a cut on his forehead, evidence of the rough fashion in which he had been persuaded to stay on board the ship. He was, Anne could see, both nervous and scared.

The other convict was older, in his mid-twenties. He was a tall, almost lanky man, with thick brown hair trimmed short with the same lack of expertise as his companion's. His dark eyes were bright, and unexpectedly intelligent, and his colouring was slightly sallow, but in spite of this, he was obviously an Englishman. Better dressed, he would have been passably goodlooking, if one excepted a scar on his chin.

For a few minutes, they had nothing to do, not having yet been fitted into the ship's routine, and as one man, they both stared at Anne as she came up on to the deck and began her measured pacing back and forth, this being her exercise and a means of passing the time which dragged so wearily.

Men had stared at Anne before, but this time she knew that it was not because of her good looks or elegance. In her crudely-coloured, badly-made shift covered against a cool breeze by Robert Laurence's jacket with the cuffs turned up, she felt that she must be a strange scarecrow. On her head was a woven palm-leaf hat, given to her by Christie, who had purchased it on shore at Tahiti. For some time now, Anne had walked barefoot about the ship, following the custom of most of the sailors, for her one pair of shoes was too precious, and too delicately fashioned, to be worn out by daily use.

She ignored the two convicts, as she always ignored all of Captain Ducaine's piratical crew, and kept on with her pacing, counting the steps to and fro under her voice, as a means of breaking the monotony. The bosun suddenly sighted the idle pair, and bellowed at them with a blast of Dutch-accented invective. Quite obviously, they had no intention of starting a two-man revolt, for they both immediately swung themselves nimbly up the rigging, with an ease which showed that they were no strangers to seafaring life. The younger one, thought Anne, watching them surreptiously, looked as if he had been decently raised, and she wondered what folly had made him a transported felon before he was past his mid-teen years.

Then she realised that the older, darker man was trying to catch her eye, and she turned quickly away, angered, and yet at the same time, curious. It was possible that the brown-haired newcomer did not realise that he was transgressing. Since the mutiny, the crew had treated her with the greatest of respect, hardly daring even to glance at her in case they brought Ducaine's anger down about themselves. They had been allowed to debauch themselves at Tahiti, but she and Christie were as securely guarded as the Golden Apostles which were hidden somewhere on board this evil ship.

Not for the first time, as she seated herself beneath the awning, she wondered where the statuettes were hidden. The mutineers had certainly been unable to find them, and, later, during *The Eagle*'s stay in Tahiti, the ship had been only lightly guarded. It puzzled Anne. The treasure was of a worth beyond imagining, but Ducaine went to no special pains to guard it.

Three days out of Tahiti, she was once again on deck when the ship passed a small flotilla of canoes strung out across the sea, each just barely within the vision of its fellows. Woven sails took advantage of the breeze, but the outrigged craft looked so small, and so frail, in comparison with the high-masted bulk of *The Eagle* that she had to marvel at the courage of the Polynesians who manned them. Even in this good weather, there was so little freeboard that baling was a constant necessity.

'They're probably the best sailors in the world.'

She knew the speaker without turning her head. The surprisingly well-educated voice belonged to the taller and older of the convicts who had been 'crimped' at Tahiti. Already, she had learned, the two newcomers had been stamped with the nicknames which were common-place with the crew. The younger was, simply, 'The Boy', whilst the other was 'Botany'. This immediately identified him as one who had served time at the notorious New South Wales penal settlements, which were all lumped, quite incorrectly, under the name Botany Bay.

She did not deign to answer his remark, but remained at the rail to watch the nearest of the canoes. There was a woman with a baby in her arms on board, and Anne waved in response to the cheerful smile, but wondered to herself how this pretty young mother felt, out of sight of land, with perhaps many miles to travel in that tiny craft.

Christie was also on deck, but seated under the awning, self-satisfied and lazy. Her presence was the reason why Anne preferred to stand. Then Botany spoke again, very softly, hardly moving his lips in the manner common amidst prisoners, obviously now aware that communication with the fair-haired hostage was forbidden the crew.

'The canoes come together at sunset. By sailing so far apart during the day, they give themselves the best possible chance of sighting land.'

He continued all the while splicing together two pieces of rope, so as not to attract the attention of his superiors. She should have walked away, but there was inside of her a desperate longing to carry on a conversation with someone who used the English language in the same way as herself. On board *The Eagle* there were several renegade Britons, but their speech was the ugly cant of the gutter, almost unintelligible to those outside the criminal class.

'What will happen if they happen to land on an island occupied by another tribe?' It worried her to think of that pretty woman with the baby running into such dangers.

'The Polynesians all speak the same language. Provided their islands are not at war, wherever they land they will be understood — unless, of course, they are unlucky enough to be blown so far off course as to find themselves in New Zealand. The Maoris seem to be at war with everyone.'

She was astonished. This felon was plainly of an enquiring and absorbent mind, and she wondered what he had done to be transported. But, as he spoke, still very quietly, his dark eyes stared into hers, momentarily, in a particular way, as if trying to impart a message, and she knew that the prime purpose of this conversation was not to impart information about the Polynesians. Before she could speak again, he moved away, with the gait of a man accustomed to life at sea.

'What did he say to you?'

This was Christie, snappingly suspicious.

Anne sat herself down, taking up a shirt which had belonged to poor Robert Laurence, and which she was altering, at Ducaine's behest, to fit Daniel the mulatto. Daniel's official duty was that of ship's carpenter, but he was always favoured in small ways, which annoyed Christie often and visibly.

'He remarked on the natives in the canoes, that's all.'

122

'The crew aren't allowed to talk to you. Captain Ducaine won't permit it.'

If you had spoken to me in that tone two months ago, thought Anne, I'd have sent you packing. But she kept her own voice mild as she repeated exactly what Botany had said. She was sure now that the convict had been trying to establish a contact with her, and although common sense told her that it could be from the most ulterior of motives, the hope of finding a friend urged her to establish that his action in speaking to her had been absolutely innocent.

'H'm. He's an odd one, that one. If I'd been the captain I'd have thrown him back on to Tahiti so's he could go on living with those heathen savages. The way that man looks and talks, you'd think he was as good as the likes of Sir Emmet Harley, but he's just a common convict, and Reverend Mr. Nott on Tahiti said that the escaped convicts on Tahiti are a real thorn in his side, the very lowest of the low.'

'In that case,' said Anne drily, 'he's found himself amongst friends.'

Christie's full red mouth tightened, and her eyes sparked angrily.

'There's a difference. Captain Ducaine's working for the Emperor, and when Bonaparte wins, things'll be different for the likes of me, you wait and see. You've never been poor, put on to the parish so's you won't starve to death. You haven't been widowed and had to go back all humble to beg to be taken in again.'

Anne was taken aback at the sheer bitterness in the other's voice, and ashamed too, of her lack of understanding for the miseries of the Christies of this world, but at the same time, she could see the faults in the other's logic.

'I'm afraid I cannot see how stealing treasure and killing harmless people — and most of those who died in Lima were killed for no reason except that they happened to be *there* — will help the poor.'

'Well, I do. When the Emperor wins over the British, there'll be justice for everyone, like there is in the United States. There'll be no more press-ganging like there was for my poor Jack.'

There was no point in arguing that poor Jack had been press-ganged because of a war started by that same Bonaparte who dazzled Ducaine. Christie now found herself in a position which offered the possibility of revenge upon a world which had treated her unfairly, and Anne was part of that world.

She decided to change the subject.

'What sort of man was Mr. Nott?' she

124

asked. She had already tried, mentally, to match up Botany's voice with that which had come to her so miraculously through the porthole at the very time when her spirits were at their lowest. Botany was definitely not the owner of that voice.

'Oh nothing very much in particular,' shrugged Christie. 'Not gentry. He could read and write, though. He was teaching that big fat King Pomare. It was funny being married out there in the open air, with all those savages watching. Some of the natives were married at the same time, though not in the Christian way, and we shared the feast. The way some of them carry on — disgraceful I call it.'

The wonder of it is, thought her companion, that Ducaine bothered to marry you. You were already his.

But, Christie's description of the Reverend Mr. Nott as 'not gentry' but educated did add weight to Anne's theory that the missionary may have been the owner of the voice. This in turn posed the question — how did the missionary learn about the captive aboard *The Eagle*? Ducaine had undoubtedly been posing as a harmless Yankee trader whilst at Tahiti, but could one of the crew have mentioned Anne to a native, who had passed it on to Mr. Nott? And could Mr. Nott have then approached Botany?

This was where the theory collapsed. Mr. Nott, according to Christie, despised and hated the escaped convicts on the island.

Christie must have mentioned that Botany was to be watched, because the next day, which was still fine, with a fair following wind, Captain Ducaine yelled out at the convict.

'You! I want a word with you!'

There was no hesitating when Ducaine called in that ferocious tone of voice. He was master of this ship, and of the lives of all thereon.

Botany jumped down lithely from the lower shrouds. Anne, sitting in her usual place under the awning, saw the fear flash across the features of his younger companion, the lad they all called 'The Boy'.

'Sir?' The response was mild, correct, and careful.

The whole crew seemed to pause in going about its duties. Boredom was setting in again after the lively interlude at Tahiti.

'Why were you sent out to Botany Bay?' The question was fired, not asked. 'You're not the usual run of convict. I've called in at Sydney more than once, and I know the breed.'

A wry and not unattractive smile creased

the other's face, and he appeared to consider carefully before answering.

'Now, captain, that's a painful subject. They do say that not one man who's been sent out under hatches to Botany Bay has been guilty of the crime for which he was convicted. No man of sense ever admits to guilt, Captain Ducaine.'

'You've a smart tongue in your head.' Ducaine's cold eyes became more chilled. 'Too smart, by far.'

'That's what *they* said, sir.'

'Well, keep that damned tongue of yours civil, or you'll find yourself at the receiving end of the cat-o'-nine-tails. Now, get back to your duties, you infernal scum.'

For an instant, just as he turned, Botany looked straight at Anne, who, during this interlude, had been holding her breath on his behalf. His face was momentarily away from both the captain and the interested onlookers, and his left eyelid flicked down very slightly. The sheer insolence of it sent the doubts whirling through her head again. Was he her friend, or merely a professional trickster? On the other hand, was that slight flicker an assurance that he was indeed her ally? Very badly, she wanted him to be the latter.

It was something to occupy her mind

during the long, lonely hours. She tried to be realistic. Criminals, after all, came in many grades. Not every man who was transported to New South Wales came from the sprawling, fetid, London rookeries where crime bred as fast as the rats under the rotten flooring. Amongst those who had to answer to the law, there was always a sprinkling of persons who had been well-educated and decently raised, who could well pass as gentlemen even if they had not been born as such. Forgers and embezzlers, by the very nature of their calling, could not be crude, ignorant, ill-lettered fellows.

There was also the unpleasant possibility that the man Botany was an habitual lecher, seeking an easy conquest. Yet, at the same time, how hard it was to quell that flutter of hope.

Like herself, Botany was on board *The Eagle* against his will.

Some time after leaving Tahiti, Ducaine altered course from due west to a direction slightly more northwesterly. Sometimes, *The Eagle* sailed quite close to groups of flat islets, the famed coral atolls of the South Seas, each almost a circle about a clear, calm lagoon. On one occasion, with a sudden softening, Ducaine lent Anne his glass, so that she could see, amidst the palm trees, the small thatched huts of the natives. It astonished her that human beings could find a living on these small islands, but the inhabitants appeared to be well fed, and the naked children running about seemed lively and healthy.

By now, the fresh food brought aboard at Tahiti was quite exhausted, but Ducaine kept his ship steadily on its chosen course, ignoring the grumbles and sullen faces of the crew. He would, it seemed, be prepared to press on to his mysterious destination in the East Indies whatever privations the ship's company suffered, but, one morning Anne awoke to find the ship at anchor in a small bay, under the shelter of a steeply rising mountain. In complete contrast to the flat atolls they had seen in such numbers, this island was an ancient volcano thrusting straight up out of the ocean, although the ubiquitous coral creatures had been busy enough to build the reef which made it possible to land on a beach which would have otherwise been lashed by surf.

Fresh water had become a pressing necessity, for there had been no rain squalls for some time, and Ducaine planned to replenish the casks here on this apparently uninhabited island. Christie, sick of being aboard ship, demanded loudly to be allowed to go ashore to stretch her legs. After some hesitation, Ducaine agreed, and then surprised Anne by suggesting that she should also go ashore for the sake of exercise.

'There's nowhere you can escape to, Miss Stacey, so don't try. The island's so small that we'll hunt you down in minutes, and if you're stupid enough to try any tricks, you'll be confined to your cabin for the rest of the voyage. Do you understand that?'

She nodded.

Oh, the joy of feeling firm ground underfoot again, even if it did take some minutes to adjust herself to a surface which did not constantly roll! The dense jungle draping itself down the steep slopes of the mountain did not tempt her, and she confined her wanderings to a walk along the strip of crunchy beach. Some of the sailors filled the water casks from a small waterfall splashing down a crevice in the rock face to the beach, whilst others gathered coconuts from a few palms growing near the water's edge, this being the only obvious food.

'Do you know where we are going?'

Anne had seated herself on a fallen trunk, and Botany, stooping to pick up coconuts, spoke so quietly that she could scarcely hear his question.

'To the East Indies,' she replied, almost

as softly, whilst pretending to draw a design in the sand with a stick.

'I know that, but can you tell me any more?'

Two other sailors approached, and she arose and walked along the edge of the water in the pretence of searching for seashells. The sand was sharp underfoot, and she regretted her shoes, left on *The Eagle*.

There was a spit, a peninsula in miniature, jutting out into the lagoon, and she ventured upon it, looking with some interest down into the water, which was fairly deep at this place. There was weed, and innumerable small fish darted through it, putting all their efforts into surviving the inexorable underwater law — escape or be eaten by the creature next up in size. Shells, still carried by their living owners, moved sluggishly on branches of coral, and a huge jellyfish propelled itself along just beneath the surface of the water. It was an odd shape, almost square.

She turned, not very interested in this underwater jungle after the first few minutes, and stood for some time regarding the scene on the beach which curved from one small headland to another. *The Eagle* rode easily about a hundred and fifty yards from the shore, and two boats were now being plied back and forth, bearing empty casks on the inward trip to be filled, returned aboard, emptied into the large casks, and then ferried back again until as much water as possible had been collected and stored. Christie sat on the beach, drying her dark curls, which she had washed beneath the waterfall, and Ducaine suddenly descended upon her and berated her for sitting in the hot tropical sun without a hat. After an angry exchange of words, in which she came off worse, Christie picked up her woven hat, the double of the one Anne wore, and thrust it back on to her head.

Then Ducaine turned his attention back to his men, telling them to hurry, for there was a streak of cloud on the horizon, and he wanted to be well away from the reef before the wind rose. It was now past noon, and the sun had dipped slightly behind the summit of the mountain, and as if on a signal from the first lowering of shadow, insects swarmed out from the undergrowth. Ducaine yelled again, this time at Botany and The Boy, who gathered dry weed into a heap and set it alight, the acrid smoke being intended to discourage the insects, which, having scented fresh blood, were not so easily deterred. Christie squealed and slapped at her arms, and demanded to be allowed to go back to the ship the very next trip.

That, thought Anne, is something which is never included in those artists' impressions of rare and remote places visited by explorers and scientific expeditions. No mosquito or vicious sandfly ever appears in those picturesque scenes. Yet, this beach was quite worthy of an artist's pen and brush. The waterfall, falling almost straight from a spring far up in the mountain, the lush green growth illuminated here and there by exotic flowers, the palms edging the beach, the white, coarse sand, the faded but still gaudy shirts worn by the seamen — all were worthy of being recreated on canvas so that armchair travellers, safely in their comfortable English homes, could marvel at the wildness and strangeness of it all.

The mulatto, Daniel, stood knee-deep in the water, helping to push one of the boats off the sand for its final trip back to *The Eagle*. Christie had just been helped in, and Anne began hurrying in response to Ducaine's summons.

Then Daniel's mouth opened in the scream he could never utter, and small noises came from his voiceless throat. His hands flailed about in his agony, and he staggered the few feet to the beach, whilst Ducaine ran forward to help him.

'Daniel!' It was a cry of grief and concern,

133

so astonishing from the cold and ruthless Ducaine that it penetrated even the panic now seizing the other sailors.

Anne ran the several yards between herself and the others, cutting her left sole, she discovered later, on a sharp piece of broken shell. In that brief space of time, the mulatto slipped from what must have been the most excruciating pain into unconsciousness.

'Daniel!' Ducaine repeated the other's name, slapping the mulatto's cheeks, vainly trying to bring him back to life.

Anne felt her elbow gripped from behind. It was Botany, who had left his bonfire.

'What are those pieces of thread on his legs?' she whispered. 'What had happened to him?'

As she watched, she could see the great red weals raising themselves on the mulatto's bare calves.

'Jellyfish,' said Botany, laconically, and Ducaine heard him, whilst from the boat, Christie demanded loudly to be told what was happening.

'Can you do anything?' demanded the captain.

'Nothing,' said the convict. 'There's a poison in those threads which kills almost immediately.'

Anne remembered the strange, box-like

jellyfish she had seen, and shuddered, averting her eyes from the dying Daniel, and suppressing a sudden nausea.

'He can't die!' Ducaine had risen to his feet, his face ashen. 'He must not die. He's my luck.'

The other boat had arrived from *The Eagle*, and its crew, jumping carefully over the bow straight on to the sand as the men realised the danger lurking in the water, now joined the frightened huddle about the dying sailor. As much as anything, they were affected by Ducaine's sombre announcement that their captain's luck was contained in the person of the mute Daniel. Superstition held as much fear for them as the perils beneath the surface of the lagoon. Of all those present, Botany was the only one unaffected by the contagion of terror which had swept through this band of assorted ruffians, and he knelt down by Daniel, feeling the pulse in the mulatto's neck.

'I'm afraid he's gone, God rest his poor soul,' he said, simply.

There was now an argument, because no one was prepared to step into the water to push the boats off, and for the time, Ducaine seemed to be in a daze. Botany then suggested, in his quiet, calm voice, that some poles be cut so that the ship's boats could be moved out in the manner of punts.

'Yes.' Ducaine was trying to recover himself. 'You and the lad. And be quick about it.'

Botany, always on the alert for opportunity, beckoned Anne.

'You can help carry them back,' he commanded, and such was the confusion over the mulatto's bizarre death that no one argued against it.

He wasted no time in coming to the point as soon as they were out of immediate earshot. He and The Boy hacked vigorously at some suitable saplings, and he spoke quietly to Anne at the same time.

'Java is under French control. Is that where Ducaine is taking the treasure?'

'I know very little.' She was still cautious, not altogether trusting his motives.

'You must try to find out more. Ask the woman.'

'I don't think that she knows very much.'

'Try, then. She must know something of his plans. We must be on the alert for a chance to escape. I've no intention of going to the gallows as a traitor to my country.'

Then he told her to drag one of the poles back to the boats. Christie was screaming and refusing to have the body in the same boat as herself, and Ducaine yelled at her and told her that she would have to do as she was told. Dragging another pole. Botany caught up with Anne.

'She must know,' he repeated, out of the side of his mouth.

The mulatto was buried at sea the following morning, and for a long time Ducaine stood watching the spot where the canvas bundle had entered the water. The unease he suffered was contagious. From that day on, the crew of *The Eagle* never seemed so confident, and there were mutterings that the Golden Apostles were wreaking a curse upon those who had snatched the statuettes on the way to their rightful place in Lima's cathedral.

11

'Miss Stacey!'

She was almost asleep, having finally arranged herself so that she could be reasonably comfortable on the hard bunk. Sleeping had become a problem: the perpetual warmth of these regions, even whilst at sea, made a good night's rest difficult. Also, leading such a sedendary and constricted life as a prisoner meant that she was never weary enough to fall asleep instantly, as she had for most of her life until that terrible day in Lima.

Now she sat up, startled, eyes accustoming to the faint illumination from the stub of candle he held.

'What are you doing here! Leave immediately!'

For answer, he touched the flame of his piece of candle to the lantern hanging from the ceiling. After all these weeks of captivity, her dread of being subjected to indignities by the crew had faded a little, but this convict from New South Wales apparently considered risking Ducaine's wrath worthwhile for a few minutes of her company.

'Ssh! I must talk to you.' Then he glanced

about and grimaced. 'Did they keep you locked up in this hole all the time the ship was at Tahiti?'

In this tropical climate, she had fallen into the habit of sleeping naked, and she kept the rough blanket up to her chin as she replied in the affirmative.

'You poor girl! It's a wonder you didn't lose your mind. Now, please don't be afraid of me. We must talk if we are to escape when the time comes.'

'They'll kill you if they catch you here.'

'Jemmy — The Boy — is keeping watch for me. He's made friends with Davey, the cabin boy — they're much of an age. Davey will tell Jemmy things he wouldn't mention to anyone else. Tonight, for instance, he let on that Mistress Christie has had too much wine and is sound asleep. Ducaine is on deck. But we mustn't waste time. Tell me everything you know about Ducaine's intentions. I know that Ducaine betrayed the Frenchman, Laurence, for his own ends, and that Laurence died in an unsuccessful mutiny before you reached Tahiti.'

'Are you planning to take the Apostles?'

He was thoughtful for a moment or two, sending her a rather ruminative glance. Then, he shook his head.

'No,' he said. 'The notion is tempting,

139

but . . . All I wish, Miss Stacey, is to escape from this hell ship, and hopefully, take young Jemmy and yourself with me. I've thought about it long and hard, and I doubt whether we can risk anything before we reach the Indies, probably the island of Java. Even if we could steal one of the boats now, we'd have a very long journey across open water before we reached Sydney. The northern part of the New South Wales coast is guarded by huge coral reefs, extending a thousand miles or so, and even if we could reach the coast directly west of our present position, we would have a long journey south to the settlements If we found ourselves cast upon any of the islands of the New Hebridies or Solomons, we would most likely be instantly massacred. No, we must wait until we reach Java, which I am almost positive is Ducaine's destination, and having obtained a boat, endeavour to make our way to Georgetown, the East India Company station on Penang. There is a chance then that we could be picked up by a British warship on the way, as Java is being blockaded by the British East India squadron.'

The very notion of travelling great distances in a small boat made her feel faint and inadequate.

'Oh, no,' she said. 'I am sure that if

Captain Ducaine does reach Java safely, and delivers the Golden Apostles to the French there, he will let me go.'

'Wait a minute. What do you mean? He intends to give the Golden Apostles to the French? Java is blockaded, Miss Stacey. There is very little chance that the treasure would ever reach France.'

'I don't know for sure, but from the way Christie has spoken, of becoming very favoured by Bonaparte, I thought that was the plan.'

'Oh.' Then he chuckled. 'The crew are all anticipating a grand sharing of spoils when they safely reach the East Indies. Still, the Apostles are not my first concern. I must escape. And don't be complacent about your own future, Miss Stacey. According to young Davey, it has been the subject of some conjecture whilst Captain Ducaine has been dining with his lady. He hopes to hold you to ransom, but if that is not practical, he may use you as a quick way of raising ready money. There's many an eastern trader, Miss Stacey, who would pay dearly for your blue eyes and fair curls, and don't you forget it. If as you say, he plans to give the treasure to the French, he will need money to share with his crew.'

His words sent a chill through her, but at

the same time, there niggled at her the idea that he was talking thus to scare her into helping him, and she could not dismiss from her mind the knowledge that he had already been convicted of at least one crime.

'Do you know any way, any way at all, by which I can work my way into Ducaine's good books?'

What had come into her mind was a sheer inspiration, prompted by the memory of poor Robert Laurence, who at the last had been her guardian angle.

Botany sounded like a gentleman. Perhaps he had a gentleman's education.

'Do you speak French? Ducaine brought Mr. Laurence with him because Mr. Laurence could speak French. Ducaine has been brought up as a Yankee — he speaks only English.'

'By all that's marvellous! Miss Stacey, you are a clever young woman. I do speak some French, not enough to pass as a native of their country, but sufficient to act as an interpreter when Captain Ducaine meets up with his French allies in the East Indies. Now, let me think. My mother came from France, that's it.'

'Did she?' Already, she was doubting her impulse in advising him. To be truthful, she could not understand why she did it, for she could find no logical reason to trust him.

'She went there on a visit, once, and came home to England again, so it is true as far as it goes.' He smiled that quick, easy smile of his, and although she could not see, for his face was in profile, she knew that his eyes must have twinkled too.

Anne, despite her misgivings, had been studying Botany quite a lot. Fight it as she willed, he attracted her very much, and it took a great deal of self-recrimination and reminding herself of her betrothal to a gallant officer to keep such errant feelings in check.

'When you have the chance, tell Mistress Christie that you heard me singing in French. I'll go now. Jemmy and I have a system of signals, and it's time for me to leave. And thank you, Miss Stacey. We'll beat them yet.'

There was no outcry, although she sat tensely for several minutes, dreading the uproar which would indicate that Botany had been caught, and when she saw him going about his duties the next morning, it was an enormous relief.

Her misgivings about Botany lingered, but, whatever his ultimate aim, he was dedicated to the undoing of Captain Ducaine, and that was sufficient reason to help him. Or so Anne told herself. Therefore, she waited for a suitable opportunity to carry out his instructions. It was afternoon before the chance came, for Christie had awakened with a headache and in a bad temper. The former servant had a decided taste for liquor, something which Anne had never before suspected, and the temptation posed by the captain's well-stocked cupboard was too much for Christie to resist.

'How strange,' said Anne, innocently. 'I heard that man they call Botany singing in French this morning.'

'Huh,' said Christie. 'I wouldn't trust that man. He reminds me of that Mr. Gillespie.'

Anne could not recall Mr. Gillespie, until Christie, who had a very good memory, prompted her. Mr. Gillespie had enjoyed quite an amount of social success in the locality of Whitestairs, Sir Emmet Harley's country residence. He was reputed to be of considerable wealth and was welcome everywhere, until one sad day when the magistrate's men had arrived, and Mr. Gillespie had been led off to languish in the cells before appearing at the next assizes on various counts of fraud and trickery. There was no fortune, only a pleasant manner and a very glib tongue, both of which were used to part people from their money so skilfully that even after it had happened they could scarcely believe it.

'That may well be,' remarked Anne coldly, 'but if the man Botany can speak French, he could be of assistance to your husband in whatever enterprise he has in mind.'

'Yes.' Christie's forehead furrowed. Already her marriage was having its ups and downs, and she could see the wisdom of pleasing her husband. 'He's going to have to talk to those Frenchies in Java so that they can help him get in touch with . . . '

She realised that her tongue was running away with her and stopped abruptly.

As *The Eagle* threaded her way cautiously between the southernmost islands of the New Hebrides chain, it seemed as though Captain Ducaine's strange assertion that Daniel had been his luck might be coming true. The winds were contrary, dropping for days at a time, so that this part of the voyage stretched into weeks of monotony and edgy nerves.

The frizzy-haired Melanesians who inhabited this area of the Pacific were an aggressive people given to cannibalism. It was rumoured that shipwreck in this region could have only one end for survivors — the cooking pits of natives eager for a variation in their diet. This theory was given weight when an approach to an apparently inhabited island in search of desperately needed fresh food was met with a show of arrows. Two shots from *The Eagle's* cannon barely creased the thick jungle, and a round of musketry met with no response. These warriors were too shrewd to show themselves, and knew that they could easily pick off anyone rash enough to venture ashore. After some consultation with his officers, Ducaine decided to be prudent.

He could not afford any more casualties.

At this stage, many of the crew were far from fit. They were suffering from poor diet, and as well, the island which had been the scene of Daniel's death had provided another, more insidious poison. The insects which had swarmed out from the vegetation so voraciously had left a legacy of ulcers after the itching bites had been scratched by dirty fingernails.

To Anne fell the task of trying to treat those ugly sores, and the ban on communications with the crew was eased. A twice daily bathing with salt water was the only remedy offering for the ulcers, but nothing really cured them, and all that could be done was to keep the raw spots clean.

It was an effort to overcome her repugnance, but Christie had flatly refused to endanger her own health, so the full brunt of the obnoxious task fell to Anne. Some of the crew were not only dirty in person, but took the opportunity to make offensive remarks, and she had to grit her teeth to continue the swabbing and bandaging. Others took her ministrations meekly and were awkwardly grateful. One night, there was a noisy brawl amidst the crew, and after that, the behaviour of those who had insulted her improved. She learnt from Jemmy, The Boy, who had a running sore on his forearm, that Botany had instigated the affair which was settled so satisfactorily.

As bad as the sores which affected many of the crew was the increasing lassitude evident in some. Captain Ducaine's decision to sail the width of the Pacific had been made when the chance of snatching the Golden Apostles had presented itself, and the ship was under-supplied for such a long voyage. Especially, the lack of provisions such as sufficient pickled cabbage and lime juice was resulting in deteriorating health right through the ship.

To Captain Ducaine, in the troubles which increasingly beset him, the one bright spot must have been the stroke of luck which had brought Botany aboard at Tahiti. The convict appeared to have recovered from his resentment at being 'crimped', and readily admitted to a working knowledge of the French language. (There were actually two native Frenchmen on *The Eagle*, but they were from Brittany, and spoke only their own Breton tongue and some broken English.)

Even better at this difficult phase of the voyage, he learned that Botany had once formed part of the crew of a survey ship out from Sydney which had been engaged in exploring the northern shores[1] of New South Wales. They were now crossing the Coral Sea, and ahead was the Torres Strait, the hundred mile width of sea between the northernmost tip of New South Wales and the southern coast of New Guinea. Ducaine had visited the East Indies formerly, to collect a cargo of pepper, but he was a stranger in these waters, and although he had charts, he doubted whether they were completely reliable.

'It seems funny to me,' said Christie, as she passed on this latest information about Botany to Anne, 'that they'd let a convict go to sea.'

Anne had to marvel at Botany's quickness of thought and tongue, which latter seemed

---

[1] Now Queensland

able to convince anyone of anything. By an unspoken mutual agreement, they had not conversed since that night in her cabin, but from time to time, Jemmy passed on discreet messages, that all was going well, that she must not lose heart, and so on.

'Oh, I believe it is true enough,' Anne replied, carelessly, not knowing in the least whether it could be true or not. 'They are very short of men in New South Wales, so the convicts are employed in every way. *That* must be how Botany learned to be a sailor.'

'I don't trust him,' insisted Christie, stubbornly, that familiar sullenness hovering about her mouth. 'The trouble is, Captain misses that Daniel. I don't. Nasty creeping creature he was, always watching and making his signs that no one but the captain could understand. He says that Daniel was his only true friend. Now that sly Botany is trying to take his place.'

When it came right down to the bottom of the matter, Anne did not trust Botany either. She saw in him an opportunist who would probably try to take the Apostles for himself. Or that is what she tried to see. The trouble was, his smile, his pleasantly open manner, and above all, an intangible something which made her heart beat just a little faster each time she saw him, were all interrupting the process of pure logic.

Ducaine was more than happy to take Botany's advice about threading *The Eagle* through the channels of the Strait, which not only was dotted with innumerable islands like stepping stones from one great land mass to the other, but also harboured many treacherous reefs. It was an anxious time, for to ensure safe passage for a ship of *The Eagle's* size, soundings had to be taken constantly. To run aground here could be quite disastrous. The tiny islands were inhabited by a handsome, warlike race, more akin in blood and culture to the Polynesians than to their Melanesian and Aboriginal neighbours. Although they traded with the mainland peoples on either side, their ferocious ways had been learnt in many centuries of surviving on their tiny specks of land strung out between strongholds of people with whom they had almost nothing in common. The Torres Strait Islanders were also cannibals and headhunters.

Happily, except for a sight of distant canoes, some smoke rising from an island, and once, a throb of drums as *The Eagle* slid by a rounded hump of land, there was little sign of the Islanders.

12

The western part of the continent lying to the south was still known as New Holland, and for a while, *The Eagle* skirted the coast of that area called Arnhem Land, named long ago by a Dutch navigator honoring the land of his birth. It was not a prepossessing coast, being low and covered with endless mangrove swamps, but the presence of praus, those seemingly clumsy craft in which the Macassans sailed so far and skilfully, indicated that at last *The Eagle* was moving into East Indian waters.

'You must trust me!'

Once again, he was in her cabin, but this time she had been prepared for his visit by a few words from Jemmy earlier that same day. She was outwardly very calm, trying hard not to betray the way in which this man, in spite of all her doubts, stirred her heart into a faster beat.

She did not answer him directly, for she was determined to ask the question which had been with her for several weeks.

'I do not know who you are. I do not know your name. The other people on this ship may be satisfied to accept you as Botany, but I am not.'

He seemed a little taken aback, but then he smiled.

'Botany Smith,' he corrected her. 'Even Captain Ducaine would not accept me without a surname.'

'Smith. I'm afraid I don't believe that.'

'All right, Miss Anne Stacey. My name is Philip Lucius Stanton. Philip Lucius — L-u-c-i-u-s. As for the Stanton — well, as you may be aware, it is a common practice amongst the criminal class to change the name, but not the letter. Hence Smith. So now you know who I am.'

Suddenly, he had hold of both her hands in his. She tried to disregard the blood pounding through her body. She had never felt like this about Anthony Bretherton. He had been a childhood friend who had turned into a dashing military man, and she had mistaken hero-worship for love, encouraged by her romantic-minded aunt. Sir Emmet Harley had been right. Anthony Bretherton had not been the right man for her.

At the same time, she knew that to yield to the overwhelming attraction from the man who held her hands would be the utmost folly. By his own admission, he was nothing but a common criminal, and whatever her

152

circumstances at the present time, she was still an English gentlewoman and an heiress. Yet, at this moment, in her uncomfortable, stuffy, cramped cabin on *The Eagle*, she knew and understood, almost blindingly, just how treacherous and illogical an organ the female heart could be. It was this same compulsion which had drawn poor Inez to her death, and silly Christie into the arms and bed of the wicked Captain Ducaine.

Philip Lucius Stanton. The very name had the ring of a gentle background, with a touch of the scholarly in the Lucius.

'My father was also named Philip,' he said, very softly, 'so I am usually called Lucius by my friends.'

'You have the speech and manner of a gentleman,' she accused, tongue running away with her. 'What happened? What did you do?'

He dropped her hands and stepped back a pace in the confined space, as if belatedly fighting this slide into intimacy.

'I was a gentleman once,' he said, almost drily. 'As for what I did — our lives take strange turns, Miss Anne Stacey. But enough of that. We have very little time. We will reach the East Indian islands within the next few days if the wind holds. It is my belief that Ducaine will seek to meet the

Governor of Java at Batavia. The last I heard, the Governor was a Dutchman and a soldier, a man called Daendals, appointed by Bonaparte. But it puzzles me. Why should Ducaine risk so much to transport the Apostles to Java. It is half a world from Europe and the Emperor. Hasn't Christie said *anything*?'

'Only that the captain hopes that the French in Java can put him in touch with someone.' Then she realised that she was saying too much and stopped.

'Java,' said Lucius, thoughtfully. After a few moments silence, he asked her to try to remember anything else which Christie might have said.

'Only that . . . Oh, it was nonsense, that Captain Ducaine would be a prince and she would be a princess before they were through.'

'So that crazy Yankee must be planning something which will really please Boney! Have you seen the statuettes?'

She shook her head.

'The ones who saw them say they're each about two feet in height, and judging by the weight, of solid gold, not to mention the jewels used as decoration. Just imagine, Miss Stacey, if we could find them and spirit them away, we'd be rich beyond belief! They'd tempt old King Croesus himself.'

In the shadowy light of the lantern swinging from its hook as *The Eagle* tossed in the swell, she saw his face, usually so calm and goodhumoured, set into grim and thoughtful lines.

'We must have fresh food,' he said, changing the subject. 'Too many of the crew are sick, and the mate and bosun are trying to persuade Ducaine that it is necessary to call into the first likely port. I think even he will agree, and that port, Miss Stacey, is where we must escape.'

The very thought made her catch her breath in fear. To attempt to escape in a small boat in the hope of reaching the settlement of Georgetown in Penang seemed to her the height of foolhardiness, and she found it hard to follow the man's reasoning. By going to a place under British jurisdiction, he laid himself and Jemmy open to arrest and a return to the penal settlement at Sydney, and she told him so.

He was close to the door, listening for Jemmy's signal that he could go up on deck, and thence back to the seaman's quarters.

'Who knows, I might find my position improved because of my service to my country,' he answered. 'And remember,

Miss Stacey, your own future is in doubt. We must act.'

Alone again, she tried to think calmly. That amazing man spoke of sailing in a small boat through unknown seas to Penang as casually as he might have spoken of travelling in a barge along an English canal. On the face of things, it seemed wiser to stay on *The Eagle*, in the hope that when the vessel reached Batavia, she would be handed over to the governor to be held until a ransom or an exchange for another prisoner could be arranged.

She tried to reassure herself thus, but she knew that she could not trust Ducaine. Earlier, Botany had warned her of the possibility that Ducaine might sell her into a bondage even worse than the one she was now experiencing. It was no use hoping that traitorous Christie would persuade her villainous husband against such a course. Even if Christie sympathised with her former mistress, she would not endanger herself by going against Ducaine's will.

Desperately, she wanted to trust Botany, for the hands which had held hers had been so strong and so reassuring in their grasp. At the same time, doubts prodded at her. Instinct was all very well, but the man who had revealed his name as Philip

156

Lucius Stanton was nothing but a convicted felon. It was hard to believe that he had no interest in the fact that she was an heiress and as such worth a large sum of money to anyone who returned her safely to the British fold.

He had declared that he was bound to try to reach Penang in order to foil Ducaine's apparent plan to place the wealth of the Apostles in Napoleon's hands. Lying on the hard and crudely constructed bunk in that airless little cabin, she knew that Philip Lucius Stanton had quite made up his mind to escape, with or without her.

Anne was tired, and confused, and out of nowhere there came to her a craving for an apple, a good, round, rosy, ripe, redcheeked English apple. In her imagination, she could even feel the sharp juiciness on her tongue. She turned over on her hard bed, and wept.

★ ★ ★

As *The Eagle* sailed close to the northern shores of the stretched-out group of the Lower Sunda Islands, Ducaine spent much time on deck, studying the coastline through his glass, and then viewing the sea with as much care. He was fully aware of the danger of meeting up with any one of the many

British naval vessels which patrolled these East Indian waters, always watching out for blockade runners, either taking cargoes to Napoleon's Europe, or bringing in military supplies to the French-controlled garrison on Java.

Another hazard in these regions was the chance of being surprised by Malay pirates. Ordinarily, *The Eagle* should have been quite capable of holding off such an attack, but Ducaine was in no mood for trouble of that sort. Too many of the crew were sick, and others were now openly discontented, asking amongst themselves when the loot would be shared. To his officers' demands that they call at the first likely port for fresh food and the chance to stretch the crew's legs, he remained adamantly opposed. It was Batavia, or nothing.

Trouble, when it came, was of an unexpected kind, and sent murmurings and mutterings through the vessel that it was true that their luck had gone when the mulatto, Daniel, had died.

With Java within sight under a calm, moonlit sky, Anne was awakened suddenly by being tossed heavily from the bunk on to the floor. It was a bruising and frightening experience, and she pulled herself upright, aware that the ship now listed badly. Yet, there was no sound of rushing wind and beating waves, only shouts from above and from within the hold.

We've foundered on a reef, she thought, and felt about for her clothes, which she pulled on with quick, trembling hands. She tried her door, which was, as usual at night, barred on the outside, and then began thumping at the timber, and calling out at the top of her voice. As she did this, she heard Christie scramble from the captain's cabin, and run, screaming, up the companionway.

'What's happened? Are we sinking?'

Ducaine's shout answered her.

'You're safe for the time being. We must have struck a spike of coral, and we're taking in water, but there's no danger at present. The pumps are working.'

'What about Miss Stacey? Will I let her out?'

Well, thought Anne grimly, leaning limply against the door, at least she had the decency to remember me.

'Leave her be. We're close inshore, and there's fishing boats all about. I don't want her escaping.'

Pushing aside the hair which clung to her moist forehead, Anne swallowed her fear, and, leaving her listening post against the

159

door, clambered on to the sloping bunk from which she had been tossed and peered out of the porthole. It was almost dawn, and the moonlight was being thrust aside by the thin grey light which turned every object into a silhouette. Ducaine was right — they were in the midst of a fleet of small fishing boats. Even as she watched, the first rays of sunlight sped across the smooth water, painting everything into instant colour. As the captain had told Christie, *The Eagle* was close to land, a land of dazzling green rising into high mountain peaks. This then, was fabled Java, the dominant island of the East Indies. To the west, along this beautiful coast, was Batavia, the capital, and Ducaine's destination, where he hoped to carry on his mysterious business with Governor Daendals, instrument of the Emperor Bonaparte.

Pumps worked constantly and partly corrected *The Eagle*'s list, but the temporary repair of tarred canvas drawn over the hole obviously would not suffice in bad weather. It was now believed that a spike of coral had thrust into the hull weeks earlier, acting as a plug, but had fallen out over the past few hours. Whatever the cause, Ducaine's fury was immense, although he had to agree to take the ship into the first likely port.

Jemmy came to Anne that day to have the

dressing on his ulcer changed. Like many others, the lad was not looking well, and badly needed the medicine of good fresh food, but he was strangely cheerful.

'Mr. Stanton says to be ready,' he muttered, barely moving his lips, for Christie sat near at hand, bored and hot, contemplating the scenery, and lazily fanning herself.

'I shall.' Anne's mind was now made up, for she knew from what she had heard Ducaine call out that morning that he would rather she drowned than escaped.

The rest of the day passed slowly, and another night. The next morning, the longboat, American flag fluttering at the stern, was sent ahead with the mate, Botany, and three other seamen to explore the possibilities of a small port marked on Ducaine's chart. Before midday, the longboat returned, and the mate reported that the area was definitely under French command. He had seen the tricolour at the head of a flagpole on shore, although there was no shipping worth mentioning in the harbour. The harbour itself was good — a deep bay protected by an island across its mouth, leaving, however, two navigable channels leading in from open water.

Ducaine then addressed his crew, all assembled on deck with the exception of those hands still in charge of the pump.

It was important, he said, that no one on shore got wind of the valuable treasure carried by *The Eagle*. Repairs had to be carried out as swiftly as possible, and he would negotiate personally the purchase of fresh food supplies. For the final success of the voyage, it was essential that the existence of the Apostles be kept secret. Once their ship was in the harbour, undergoing repairs, they would be at a serious disadvantage, and he did not want any whipper-snapper of an officer getting it into his head that *The Eagle* was easy prey.

The men's faces reflected their dissatisfaction and unease. Too many months had elapsed since the excitement and success of the Lima raid, and they could not be blamed for wanting to hear something definite about the sharing out of the spoils.

The mate, his formerly chubby face now thin and sallow, was the one who voiced the doubts, urged on by some muttering and nudging from those standing near him.

'Beggin' pardon, cap'n,' he said, 'but where are the idols? They came on board, we all know that, but where are they now?'

'Safe!' snapped Ducaine. 'That's all you need to know.'

He raised his voice. 'Now get about your

duties, the lot of ye, or I'll clap the laggards in irons.'

For a few seconds, there was a wavering, but Ducaine still held the command. There were sullen glares, and a hint of aggressiveness amidst one knot of men, but Anne, seated under her awning, saw Botany's lips move, and obviously whatever it was he muttered calmed them, and they dispersed about their duties.

Christie came up on deck with an armful of blankets for airing. She saw Anne, and shouted at her.

'Give me a hand, lazybones, and while the sun's shinin' you'd best bring up your own bedclothes.'

Ducaine turned.

'I want her out of sight! There's too many small boats about, and I don't want her seen.'

'She could be helping me.'

'She's to go below.'

Anne went with an outward show of meekness. She did not wish to become embroiled in a domestic tiff, and even found some satisfaction from these signs that the honeymoon was definitely over.

Out of the fresh air, it was almost unbearably close, and to obtain relief, she sat herself on the bunk and stared out of the porthole. *The Eagle* had now entered the more easterly of the two channels leading to the port, and she could see the terraced rice fields rising behind the intensely green vegetation of a low, narrow coastal strip. Everywhere, there were signs of a large population, many small boats on the water, and many thatched houses on the land. These Javanese people were predominantly of Malay origin, and as typified by the men out fishing, who kept their heads covered at all times by gaily coloured cloths twisted into flat turbans, were mostly of the Moslem faith.

Anne noticed that in many of the small boats they passed, the fishermen appeared to be either rather elderly or scarcely more than children, and there were few smiles, or waves, to greet *The Eagle* as the vessel, still listing, moved a little erratically into the sheltered waters of a large bay.

She did not know it at that time, but as *The Eagle* dropped anchor about two hundred yards out from the crude jetty which served as landing place and wharf, the French commander in that area was preparing to welcome the visitors.

13

Colonel Renaud was a pleasant man in ordinary circumstances, and considering his amiable nature, it was unfortunate that the local people regarded him with the hatred they felt for all the French military men who had been sent to Java to hold the island as a Napoleonic stronghold in the East. Renaud had not lived up to early promise shown in Napoleon's first campaigns, and he would have been a fool if he had not been aware that this posting to Java amounted to a sort of exile for also-rans.

In his way, he was indicative of an essential difference between French and British outlooks. England tended to send her best men overseas, whilst Bonaparte preferred to keep his ablest lieutenants close at hand.

Still, it was hoped that Java would prove to be the springboard for a French re-entry into India, and Daendals, the Dutchman appointed by Bonaparte as both governor and commander-in-chief, had brought about the construction of an excellent road from the west to east of Java. This had improved vastly

Java's capabilities as a fortress-island, but the French officers charged with raising an army had aroused resentment by conscripting the young natives into badly-run, badly-equipped units, robbing the villages of their best workers.

Renaud made the best of a bad job, although he regarded the local brown-skinned people with a tolerant contempt. They were lazy, hopeless at drill, and he would not trust them past the end of his nose, but he had to admit that some of the women were quite attractive, in spite of their vile habit of chewing the betel which stained their teeth and lips. Dark women were not altogether to his taste, although the Eurasian girl who had been added to his household was pleasant enough in her uncultivated fashion. He loathed the heat, and his one real joy in this outpost was his boat, *L'Esprit*, the smart little craft in which he had been sailing when *The Eagle* hove into sight.

Astonishment at seeing an American flag was replaced by hope, which had been low lately since the news that both Indian Ocean islands of Mauritius and Reunion had been lost to the British. Could this mean that the blockade which had been strangling Java was no more? Had England been defeated at last?

Within minutes he was within hailing distance of the ship, and Ducaine, as Anne heard from her prison, immediately yelled out for Botany. (Strange, how she still thought of Stanton by that name.)

'Where's that damned convict? At the pumps? Send him up at once!'

Colonel Renaud lost no time in coming on board.

What luck that he had been out sailing so that he could hear the latest news first hand! He sailed, he said, 'a mes heures perdues', but listeners could have been forgiven for thinking that his odd moments were long and often. He was, dieu merci, a good sailor, or he would have gone out of his mind in this hole of a place. At least, on the water, it was not so unbearably hot.

He announced himself overjoyed to see an American ship in these waters, and although disappointed to learn that Ducaine had no news from Europe, he was full of praise on hearing that *The Eagle* had cheated the British blockade by coming in from the east instead of the more likely directions.

He knew that His Excellency in Batavia would welcome Ducaine with open arms. Trade had dropped away to nothing recently, and Java was almost bankrupt, he said, sinking gratefully on to the chair under the awning usually reserved for Anne.

'Oh, how I envy you the seafaring life,' he declared, whilst Botany did his best to translate the voluble Frenchman's rapid speech. 'The heat on land is intolerable. And that smelly little town! Nothing to entertain one except cock fighting. Ah, c'est la guerre.'

'Tell him we have to repair the ship,' said Ducaine, angry at himself for not being able to talk directly to the visitor.

Renaud declared that he would do everything to help, but he admitted to curiosity about Captain Ducaine's presence here. Did it mean that at last the citizens of the United States had decided to support their brothers-in-revolution? Did he perhaps have munitions to trade?

Ducaine asked Botany to tell the Frenchman that he could rest assured that the materials needed for repairs would be paid for, as would the fresh food the crew needed so badly. Now a frown creased the Frenchman's sun-reddened face.

That would be difficult. So many of the natives were in the armies, being trained — not that they were any good — and there was actually a food shortage in this lush and fertile land. He would, however, do what he could.

168

Already a certain disappointment was showing through his amiability.

'Tell him we'll do the actual repairs,' added Ducaine. 'All we need is some good, seasoned timber.'

Botany's French was no means as fluent as he had made out, and now Renaud made a suggestion. His aide, Lieutenant L'Estrange, spoke passable English, having lived in India as a youth, and there been a prisoner of the British for some time after the defeat of the French-Indian forces. Would Ducaine and his lady — for Christie hovered on the edge of the group — care to dine ashore with himself and the lieutenant that same evening?

After the invitation had been accepted, he said that it was a joyful occasion to meet with an American, a citizen of the country whose own fight for freedom had inspired France's glorious revolution, the noble principles of which were being applied here in this backward land of Java. He knew in his heart that the Americans, short of actual war, were doing everything possible to help the French cause.

It was not hard to guess that, beneath the flowery phrases, the colonel was doing some fishing, for Ducaine had not once admitted his reasons for being in Javanese seas.

Anne heard about Renaud's visit from Christie who, excited at the idea of her first real dinner party as Mrs. Ducaine, commanded that the other should help dress her hair. Anne's first instinct was to refuse, but then sense dictated that it would be wise to take this order good-humouredly, although she did point out that she had little skill in the arts of tire-woman.

'I'll tell you what I want,' replied Christie, imperiously.

She was now of a flutter over what she would wear, and without a by-your-leave, took out Anne's precious gown, relic of that last day in Lima. Regretfully, she put it aside as she realised that she could not have fitted into it without splitting a seam. She despised her own simple cotton dress as a memento of her serving days, but in the end accepted that it was more flattering than the brightly coloured homemade shifts cut from gaudy trade stuffs. Anne, wishing to keep Christie in a pleasant mood, for she hoped to hear some snippets of information about the dinner party, suggested that the other should borrow one of Captain Ducaine's silk sashes. This was an inspiration, and considerably smartened the plain garment.

'We're taking that convict Botany with us,' said Christie, casually. 'The Frenchie said that his aide can speak English, but Peter doesn't trust them above half, and he hopes Botany can tell him what they say between themselves.'

Anne had to keep her fingers from trembling as she carefully plaited Christie's flowing and untrimmed black hair so that it could be braided neatly about her crown. Lucius Stanton's audacity constantly amazed her, and despite the humid heat in the cabin, a sense of chill passed through her as she thought of what might happen if Ducaine discovered that the convict, despite his past, was still fervently loyal to flag and country. She knew too, that any time now, Lucius Stanton would seek the opportunity for their escape, and she silently prayed that when the moment came, her own courage would not fail.

'I'm going to ask one of those Frenchies to take me to the shops in the town,' continued Christie, after complaining that Anne was drawing her hair too tight. 'They're sure to have combs and ribbons and perhaps some Indian stuffs so as I can have a decent gown or two to wear when we meet the governor in Batavia. I don't fancy looking a frump.'

I could do with some odds and ends myself, thought Anne, but kept her peace.

'I do not care for the notion of being left

on board without the captain's protection,' she said, after a few minutes.

'He'll put a padlock on the outside of your door, same as he did in Tahiti,' answered Christie, as if it were of no account.

'When am I going to be set free?'

Christie's face developed a sly look, and obviously the question had surprised her.

'Soon,' she said, after a brief mulling.

Her very hesitation convinced Anne that what Stanton had suggested earlier could well be true. If no other way of using her for a profit eventuated, Ducaine could well sell her to a slave trader.

'It will be good to be home again,' Anne stated, as evenly as she could. 'Don't you want to see England again, Christie?'

'What, be poor again, and have you send me to prison perhaps?' Christie snorted with laughter. 'What do you take me for, a fool?' Then she smiled, very smugly. 'I can tell you this, when Boney's won the war, if Peter and me get the fancy, we *might* go to London, and the Prince of Wales 'll be glad to welcome us.'

'I can't see how giving the Apostles to the French here in Java will help Bonaparte win the war!'

'But that's not what Peter's planning.'

Christie realised that she had said too

much, but Anne shrugged as if it did not matter. The cat had not been let out of the bag, but at least a nose and a whisker or two had been revealed.

That evening, after Ducaine, Christie and Botany had been rowed ashore, it seemed to Anne that there was rather more scurrying and muttering about the ship than usual. She felt a wretchedness which was rather more than the usual misery of being locked into the cabin. Her head ached increasingly, and she was very thirsty. Very late, she heard the captain's party return from shore, and the sound of Lucius Stanton's voice raised in tipsy song.

Disillusionment swept through her. She depended so much on the man, and in fact, had woven stupid, romantic little stories about him to herself. Now, it was obvious, he had a weakness which could easily betray him — and herself.

Not for the first time, she cried herself to sleep.

The following morning, Christie ordered her to dress herself in her good gown and to go immediately up on deck. Already, Anne had left her breakfast, which was actually the best and most palatable she had seen for a long time, being *real* bread (sent on board by Colonel Renaud), fresh eggs, and fruit.

Her headache had worsened, but partly from a lack of desire to argue, and partly from a conviction that, once she went up into the fresh air and moved about a little, she would feel better, she forced herself to dress.

'And put your shoes on,' said Christie, lolling at the door. 'Captain says you're to be dressed proper.'

Anne had gone barefoot for so long that her shoes pinched and felt awkward on her feet, and slippery on the rungs of the companionway.

Ducaine was waiting for her, and she saw a somewhat worried-looking Botany in the background. Well might you look so sad and sorry, she thought contemptuously, and refused to catch his eye.

This was the first time she had seen their anchorage in its entirety, and she was surprised by the size of the town which sprawled behind the shores. Most of the buildings were low, wooden, and haphazardly arranged, with little sign of formal town planning. On rising ground to one side of the harbour, there was a group of fairly large stone buildings within a walled enclosure, with park-like grounds running down to the beach, where there was a small jetty. This was the former palace of a minor prince who had ruled the region under Dutch

174

suzerainity until the French had assumed military command. Colonel Renaud used the palace buildings as his headquarters, and he found this particularly convenient as it meant that his prized *L'Esprit* was no more than a stroll away at the jetty.

The harbour itself was alive with small craft, the occupants of which, in many cases, were eager to sell their goods to *The Eagle*. Ducaine constantly ordered them away, and he had finished an exchange with a particularly persistent Chinese woman trader when he saw Anne approach.

'You've become thin!' he accused, surveying the girl up and down, as if her loss of weight had been contrived to annoy him.

'What do you expect?' she countered. 'My rations have been cut along with everyone else's, and much of the time, the food isn't fit for a pig to eat.'

'Now you know how common folk fare,' jeered Ducaine. Then: 'Rub your cheeks, woman, and look a mite more healthy!'

She chose to ignore this somewhat puzzling command by turning on her heel and walking away. Angered, the captain grabbed her arm and pulled her back before forcefully rubbing the knuckles of his left hand against the skin under her cheekbones. She bit him, and he let her go.

'You bitch!' he said. 'I should've done what I wanted to in the first place and fed you to the sharks.'

Violently, he pushed her so that she fell into the chair beneath the awning.

'Now, listen,' he continued, 'you'd best behave yourself, my fine lady, because our French friends have offered to take you off my hands for the sake of whatever ransom they can raise.'

She was appalled by this new development. All the while, she had thought herself safe until they reached Batavia. Instinctively, she looked about for Botany, but he was no longer in view. Yet, could she depend upon him at all? He had been so full of talk about escaping, and his duty, but he had put up little resistance to French hospitality the previous evening.

'Let her be!' It was a rough voice, belonging to a seaman, above them in the shrouds.

If this command had come directly from heaven, Ducaine could not have been more astonished, but he soon recovered himself, and in a bellowing voice, demanded that the man, whom Anne knew as one of the worst characters on board, come down immediately. Then he called out loudly to the mate to come and clap the fellow in irons.

A hush fell over *The Eagle*, and the man above did not budge.

'The lady's been good to many of us,' he said. 'She's dressed our sores when that high and mighty strumpet wouldn't touch us.'

Ducaine pulled out the pistol he always carried thrust into his sash, and pointed it upwards towards the miscreant, who dropped agilely down, and then across a spar, hoisting himself up in a cross-wise direction, moving so quickly that Ducaine could not take aim. Now, with the exception of those still working the pumps below, the whole crew gathered on the deck.

Unnoticed, the little *L'Esprit* had left her moorings, and was skimming out towards *The Eagle*, with both Renaud and his aide, L'Estrange, on board.

14

As she described the events of that day to the lawyer, who much of the time looked as much bored as interested, Anne could remember the scene as vividly as if it had been entrusted to canvas and then shown before her eyes. Oddly, she could even see herself, sitting frightened in her chair, the once-elegant gown hanging a little loosely upon her, slim arms browned by exposure, and her hair bleached and unruly. Although she felt feverish and ill, she was very pale, except for the marks of Ducaine's knuckles upon her cheeks, and almost hollow-eyed. It was little wonder, when she thought about it later, that Ducaine had been so angered by her appearance, for, as she now knew, he had arranged with the French commandant that he should exchange his valuable hostage for supplies.

Forward, the men congregated in a line across the width of the ship, with the mate standing slightly in front of them. He was a swarthy, almost yellow-skinned man called Tarrago. Mr. Tarrago. It was a strange name, and she did not have the slightest idea of his origins or nationality. He had an accent of some kind, but it did not seem to fit any particular country or language.

'We won't have you giving the lady over to that Frenchie,' the mate said. 'She's done us no harm, and if there's any giving over to be done, it's to the governor hisself in Batavia.'

Approval murmured through the rest of the crew.

'Scum!' roared Ducaine, but this time there was a hollowness in his tone, as if some of his confidence was leaving him.

At the time of the first mutiny, he had known that most of the men were on his side, but just as his belief in his luck had faltered when the one he had believed to be his talisman, the mulatto Daniel, had died, so had that of his crew.

'Back to your work,' he continued. 'We need planks for the repairs and food for your rotten carcasses. If they'll take the woman to hold her to ransom, why should we part with our treasure?'

'Where is the treasure?'

It was Botany who asked the question, mildly, but in a clear voice.

Ducaine still held the pistol limply at his side, and now he raised it, aiming directly at Botany.

'You're the one!' he cried. 'You're the one who let on what was spoken in secret last night, for all that you were far gone in wine. I should 'a' listened to Daniel. He told me that you were a curse on the ship. He had ways of knowing these things. And my wife. She's warned me again and again about you, that you're the worst, a gentleman who's gone to the bad.'

Christie had come up on deck, and stood quietly near Anne, bracing herself with one hand on the taffrail. Her eyes had opened very wide, and she bit at her lower lip nervously.

'She's not your wife,' said Botany, slowly and clearly. 'You've a legal wife in Maine.'

'Yeah, that's so,' said one of the seamen, nodding in agreement, and Christie screamed, and hurled herself at Ducaine, knocking him off balance so that they both fell to the deck.

The two French officers had hauled themselves on board, and were confronted by the spectacle of the captain and Christie rolling about in combat, whilst the mate stepped forward and picked up Ducaine's pistol.

'Clap 'im in irons,' he ordered two grinning crew members. 'And lock 'er in Miss Stacey's cabin. I'm takin' over cap'n's cabin.'

180

He turned to the astounded new arrivals and tapped his forehead significantly.

'Captain Ducaine's not fit any longer.'

'Monsieur Smith!' Colonel Renaud, who, rather to Anne's surprise, was a tall, fair man with a florid complexion, spoke up indignantly in his own language, and the other French officer, who was undoubtedly Lieutenant L'Estrange, took over in English.

'Monsieur Smith, be so good as to explain. We came in good faith to collect Mademoiselle Stacey. That was our arrangement.'

'No more,' said Mr. Tarrago before Botany could say a word. 'Miss Stacey's not for sale, and it bein' right on the tide, we're uppin' anchor and on our way. It strikes me we can find food and timber elsewhere, seein' we have two French officers to trade.'

So saying, he roared with laughter, echoed by his fellow-mutineers, who, after weeks of uncertainty and melancholy, were now seized by a new enthusiasm and vigour.

L'Estrange turned to Anne. He was, she thought, a decent looking man, and his manner was at once both bemused and apologetic.

'Mademoiselle,' he said, quickly, 'please believe that we meant you no harm. To take you in the hope of obtaining a ransom, or at least an exchange for one of our own held prisoner by the British, seemed to be in your own best interests. We were shocked to hear of your predicament.'

She believed him, but events had swept them all forward.

The two Frenchmen were told that they would have to remain on board until *The Eagle* was safely in open water. Then they would be placed on the little boat and set free. Ducaine and Christie were imprisoned below, but Anne was permitted to remain on deck as canvas was raised and the vessel, still alist and without the supplies so badly needed, headed out to sea through the more westerly of the two channels which separated the mainland from the island protecting the harbour.

At last, Botany spoke to Anne as, still somewhat dazed and feeling increasingly unwell, she watched the town recede behind them.

'Last night,' he said, very softly, 'I learned of Ducaine's true purpose in coming to Java. He intended to enlist the aid of the French here to use the Apostles to finance a new uprising in India. I feigned drunkenness so that Ducaine would talk more freely to L'Estrange. When we returned to the ship, I lost no time to telling this to the mate. The crew aren't interested in helping the French, or anyone else. They're pirates, and they want their share of the loot.'

She expressed her own fears.

'And what will happen to me now!' she asked. 'I would have greatly preferred to have been handed over to the French than risk another voyage on this terrible ship. I am sure that the Frenchmen are men of honour.'

'The French are not popular with the natives, and the town is full of fever. Trust me, Miss Stacey.'

It seemed to her that far from being trustworthy, he had placed her in worse danger than ever.

'The ship could sink.'

'Not at present. *The Eagle* will be beached on a small island somewhere, and repaired. The damage is not extensive. But do not worry about that, Miss Stacey. By then, we'll be on our way to Penang, and the men 'll be pulling this poor ship apart looking for the Apostles.'

As he spoke, he grinned, and his eyes sparkled as if at a private joke.

'The colonel's little boat will have to have some provisions and water placed aboard so that they can make their way safely back. I shall see to that myself.'

With that, he left her, and she stared at

L'Esprit, bobbing after *The Eagle* like a cygnet after mother swan. Lucius Stanton, alias Botany Smith, was crazy to believe that she would entrust herself to be taken to Penang, hundreds of miles away, on such a tiny craft.

But that was the whole story. Everyone connected with *The Eagle* was crazy, Robert Laurence-Laurent who had engineered the raid on Lima and died for it, Ducaine with his mad dreams to wresting India from the British, Christie who saw herself as a princess, and Lucius Stanton who was obsessed with escaping, although if he were successful, he could easily find himself back in the penal settlement at Sydney. They were all crazy, right down to the humblest member of the crew, taking their limping ship out to open sea so that, at last, they could share out the great wealth hidden somewhere on board.

Very much, she would have liked to have lain down, to ease her aching head, but Christie occupied her cabin now, and until fresh arrangements were made, she had to stay on deck. In an endeavour to offset the misery of her throbbing head, she tried hard to concentrate upon what Botany had told her.

India had been deemed secure since the

campaign against the ferocious Tippoo Sahib, 'le citoyen Tippou', had ended French hopes in the sub-continent. That was a decade before, and all Anne could really remember about it was that Tippoo was reputed to have a favourite clockwork toy which was in the form of a tiger tearing an Englishman to pieces.

However, her life as Sir Emmet Harley's ward had taught her that Britain was being drained dry by the long war, and more especially by Bonaparte's 'continental system', which prevented European countries from buying goods from France's island enemy. Another war in India would not only deplete those British forces fighting so desperately in Spain; it could well spell complete collapse for a country relying very much on profits from the East India Company.

If Lucius Stanton had not been a felon, she thought, Sir Emmet Harley's would have approved of him. There was about him that same ruthlessness and acceptance of the fact that others' welfare had to be sacrificed to the greater need. Whatever Stanton said, she felt sure that she would have been better off on shore with the French.

Her misgivings were soon lent weight, for without Ducaine's iron control, the crew of

The Eagle rapidly degenerated into a rabble. Someone had broached the rum casks, and an argument started about *L'Esprit*. Some wanted to cut the tow rope. They were not interested in the courtesies of war. The Frenchmen were surplus cargo to be tossed overboard or dumped on a desert isle. Sent back to their base, they could easily alert their own forces and send a warship after *The Eagle*.

Botany, his cool head as usual coping with each problem as it came, pointed out that the small craft could be of good use further on, as it could be bartered on one of the other islands for the food they needed. Anne, under her awning, stayed still and quiet, praying that Stanton would engineer their escape before the ruffianly crew forgot their respect for her.

The Eagle was by now passing through the westerly channel betwixt the island and the Javanese mainland. There was little of the cultivation evident near the town, but the grey masonry of an ancient and ruined temple perched on a natural platform high above the coastal jungle. A cone-shaped hill rising several hundred feet in the centre gave evidence of volcanic origin, and although the island did not appear to be inhabited, smoke from huts hidden amidst the dense growth showed that there were people living there.

The argument about the fate of the two French officers continued as *The Eagle* lurched into open water, and the pair were brought up on to deck. Anne felt afraid for them. They appeared to be decent men, and enemies or not, they deserved better than to find themselves at the mercy of pirates. The mate wished to set them adrift in the skiff before land fell too far astern, but the bulk of the crew, eager only for the opportunity to ransack the vessel in search of the Apostles, had other ideas.

'Throw 'em overboard!' shouted someone. 'Dead men don't tell no tales!'

It was at this instant, while the two Frenchmen stood expressionless with hands bound behind them, that Jemmy came running from the forecastle.

'Fire!' he cried, and as if to corroborate this most dreaded of all alarms, smoke billowed upwards from a hatch.

There was instant confusion, and the mate, calling to the helmsman to hold the ship steady, ran to inspect the fire himself. It was amazingly well-established, having spread far in a few minutes.

This is the end, thought Anne. She had lost all will to move, although she could see smoke already wisping up from the companionway leading down to her own cabin, now Christie's prison. Christie, the bigamous wife, was treacherous and unpredictable, but she deserved better than death in a fire. But she felt too weak to move.

Then Botany had her hands, and was pulling her from the chair, while smoke, choking and acrid, made her eyes smart.

'We can't leave Christie,' she cried, but he was forcing her over the rail, telling her to jump down into *L'Esprit*, now bobbing up and down right against the hull, for the rope had been drawn in and hitched.

'I can't, I can't,' she cried, whilst in the fore part of *The Eagle*, flames were already roaring upwards into the rigging.

Stanton lifted her up and over, so that she had to clutch at the rope, and lower herself, inexpertly, so that her hands were seared, and her joints wrenched. Jemmy, already in the small boat, reached up and helped her.

'One moment,' called Stanton from above. 'I'll free the Frenchmen.'

Then he was swinging himself down expertly, and cutting the rope with his knife, whilst Jemmy pushed '*L'Esprit*' clear.

'And what happened then,' prompted the barrister, for Anne fell silent. 'Wasn't any attempt made to recover the Apostles?'

She shook her head.

'My companions were intent only on escape,' she said. 'As we looked back, we could see aught but smoke, and many small boats approaching from the mainland.'

Recounting her story had been a tremendous ordeal, although of course she had omitted those parts concerning her own yearnings and follies regarding the man who was both Botany Smith and Lucius Stanton.

'We've beaten them, Mr. Stanton,' said Jemmy, holding the tiller and grinning like a monkey. 'I didn't expect the fire to spread so quickly, though. Much as I could do to get away without being singed, Mr. Stanton.'

'You're a good lad,' replied Stanton. 'And now, with God's help, we're on our way to Penang.'

With that, he began laughing in the exhilaration of hard-won freedom as the off-land breeze caught the sails and sent the small boat scudding across the lightly tossing sea.

'Farewell!' he cried. 'Sort it all out amongst yourselves!'

Anne said nothing. She felt too ill.

Therefore, she could tell very little of the last part of her tribulation, for the voyage off the northern shore of Java was but hazily recollected. Vaguely, she remembered brief times when she had lain on sand beneath

189

shady trees, and Botany had bathed her face with cool, fresh water and helped her to drink. He had been so kind, so gentle, and she knew that she had been a very great hindrance.

Once, she had been delirious for hours, and Stanton and Jemmy had taken it in turns to hold her for she had been impelled to jump from the boat into the sea. Then, the fever had broken, and she had fallen asleep, to awake — how many hours later? — on a British ship bound for Malacca.

L'Esprit's course had unexpectedly crossed that of the huge British invasion fleet on its way to surprise and take Java. At that time of the year, the French-Dutch forces could reasonably have considered themselves safe, for the winds were not favourable for any vessel approaching from the direction of the Bay of Bengal. But Governor Daendals reckoned without superb British seamanship. The great fleet, carrying an army of well-trained Indian troops under British officers, and with the Governor-General of India, Lord Minto, as commander-in-chief, had left Malacca into the face of trade winds, to thread its way through the Straits of Singapore and then along the sheltered side of Sumatra.

She had no knowledge of what had

happened to Botany and his faithful young helpmate, Jemmy. She herself had been taken aboard a small vessel which was being sent back to Malacca with despatches describing the first, successful part of the invasion.

'Our newspapers reported yesterday that Batavia had been captured and that all Java is now securely in British hands,' remarked the legal man who had been listening to her tale so intently. He sounded bored. 'Only a small column. There is so much of importance happening in Europe. Lord Minto returned almost immediately to India, leaving a Mr. Thomas Raffles as administrator of Java. No-one has ever heard of the man. I gather that he is an employee of the East India Company. Still, I daresay all with interests in India are vastly relieved.'

'It could have been a different story if Captain Ducaine had managed to smuggle the Apostles to those princes in India still eager to support the French,' she reminded him.

'Ah yes.' He was not much interested in supposition. 'Miss Stacey, what I am to say may offend your susceptibilities, but I must know the truth. During your whole time on *The Eagle*, you were not — ahem — abused?'

She felt her cheeks colour.

'Captain Ducaine was anxious to preserve my worth as a hostage,' she retorted.

'He would have had — um — no doubt as to your virtue? Remember, Miss Stacey, that much of Sir Emmet Harley's case against you rests on his belief that you and Robert Laurence — or Laurent — were lovers.'

'We did not care in the least for one another. I believe that Mr. Laurence truly loved Lady Harley, and in fact, as I have told you, her name was the last thing he uttered.'

Pouched but keen eyes brooded for a few seconds, and then he sighed.

'You are in a very difficult situation,' he said, and she suspected that he was stifling a yawn. 'Whilst you have been out of Britain, Miss Stacey, the lower classes have suffered greatly because of the war. Our government has been forced to take increasingly repressive measures against those poor ignorant souls who blame machines and not Bonaparte for their troubles. Here in London, the poor daily see the rich going about their pleasures as never before. They are more than happy to seize upon the adventures of a traitress as a subject for their broadside ballads.'

Then, his voice became more sympathetic.

'I have not been idle,' he continued. 'I

have put a trusted man to work trying to ascertain the state of Sir Emmet Harley's affairs. It has not been unknown that men will go to the greatest lengths to gain control of another's fortune when their own finances are askew. My other endeavours will be to set about immediately to have the convicts Lucius Stanton and Jemmy Thomas returned to Britain. This may take up to a year, or even more, and I propose to place before a magistrate that you be placed in your uncle's care until such time as a trial can be properly held.'

Seeing the hope on her face, he frowned.

'I've said too much,' he told her, 'and perhaps I have raised your hopes too high.'

'Philip Lucius Stanton,' she reminded him. 'He told me that his father was also Philip, so that he himself was usually called Lucius.'

She was so certain that her troubles, if not over, were on the way to being solved, that when the blow came, it was all the more severe.

No man of the name Philip Lucius Stanton had ever been convicted and transported to New South Wales.

He had lied to her about his name, very convincingly, but nonetheless, he had lied.

'You must realise, Miss Stacey, that this is extremely serious. The fact that there was a convicted felon of that name would have been very much in our favour. And, I am afraid, neither has a youth of the name James Thomas been transported. There are two James Thomas's listed as having been sent to New South Wales, but they are both much older men.'

15

Mr. Bretherton brought the news that his son, Major Anthony Bretherton, had been wounded at the taking of the Spanish fortress-town of Badojoz. A bone in his right ankle had been broken, and the injury being slow in healing, he was returning to England on furlough.

Listening to this, Anne waited in vain for the familiar quickening of hearbeat which had once accompanied the mere mention of Anthony's name. She was truly concerned that he had been wounded, and thankful that he had survived such a frightful battle, but her sympathy was merely for an old friend. She realised, of course, that Anthony's return would complicate affairs. Being the gallant young man he was, there was no doubt that he would come to her support. She had known for a long time that the romantic impulse which had led her to agree to marry him had been nothing but infatuation of a fleeting kind. At the same time, she was aware that, in the event of her being found guilty, her closeness to the Bretherton family would do them no good.

She found it impossible to express her gratitude towards Mr. Bretherton. If only her father had chosen to make him her guardian, how different her life would have been! A man-about-town M.P. noted for his malicious wit had gone out of his way on one occasion to count up the times — not including his maiden speech — that Mr. Bretherton had actually stood up in the House and opened his mouth. Five times, he declared, in fifteen years, and three of those times consisted of agreeing with another member. But Anne knew that Mr. Bretherton, unlike many who considered a place in the House of Commons as either a theatre for rhetoric or an opportunity for self-advancement, worked hard for the welfare of those living in his constituency, whether or not they were entitled to vote.

He was not a brilliant man, but one with solid virtues, and when the time came, loyalty. Still, Anne sensed that there had to be a limit to imposition upon his worthiness and goodness of heart.

'You must rest assured,' Anne said, in a low voice, 'that I do not consider Tony bound to me in any way. Our engagement was never formally announced.'

'Let him be the judge of that,' the man replied, gruffly, but she could not but imagine that there was the smallest hint of relief in his face.

He had done everything possible to help her, but Tony was, after all, his only son.

'But you must not lose heart,' he continued. 'Your aunt and I and the girls all believe in your innocence. Anne, I've known you since you were a child. How could I believe that you actively conspired against your country, especially when you were betrothed to a young man fighting against Bonaparte?'

'Thank you.'

The two words were simple, but from her heart. Tomorrow she would go from this place to face a court, with no defence except her own innocence.

'I went last week to Whitestairs,' continued Mr. Bretherton, 'to see Emmet Harley face to face, and to endeavour to persuade him to drop his charges against you. I was turned away at the gate. It seems that he is too sick to receive visitors, yet not too sick to make these monstrous accusations!'

With that, he left her.

When she was taken to the court, both the curious and the vindictive were out to see the heiress who had helped the French steal a fabulous treasure from Britain's Spanish allies. Catcalls, thrown garbage, and filthy remarks followed her passage in a closed

197

carriage, and the broadside-sheet vendors were out, eagerly promoting their hastily printed doggerel.

'A penny for the Ballad o' Miss Stacey and the Pirates!'

At the last moment before being led into the courtroom, she grasped the barrister's arm.

'Will I be hanged in public?'

His roué's face, unfamiliar and slightly comic under its outmoded white peruke, tried hard to smile.

'Remember all I've told you,' he whispered.

Ah yes, she had to look demure, and endeavour to weep at the appropriate time. Simple feminine wiles sometimes had been known to work in the defendant's favour. For his part, he still intended to persuade the court to delay proceedings until such time as there could be obtained information regarding the fate and identities of the two men with whom she had escaped from *The Eagle*.

How crowded the courtroom was, with its lawyers and clerks and avid sightseers, some of whom had been waiting for hours to gain entrance to the public gallery. She was shocked to see that the curious were not street rabble, but members of fashionable society, dressed in the height of style, and with quizzing glasses held high to examine her whole appearance.

Her legal adviser had told her to wear blue. It was, he said, a colour associated with virtue, and besides, the most flattering to her colouring. She had obeyed, and with her delicate loveliness so enhanced, it was little wonder that male onlookers were already softening in their opinion of her, whilst their female counterparts were labelling her as brazen.

Then, with astonishment, she saw two people she had certainly never expected to lay eyes on again, let alone find in this stuffy courtroom on an English summer day. Rosina, Inez's handsome part-Indian maid, and her equally handsome brother, Francisco, who had been servant to Robert Laurence sat stiffly on a bench reserved for witnesses. They were both surprisingly well-dressed in the English style, and their exotic appearance had already attracted some attention from the public gallery, and one beau settled down to ogling Rosina determinedly. However, the Peruvian pair remained stonily indifferent to anyone and everything but Anne, much to her discomfort.

Within the hour, she was to discover the purpose of their presence here. They were now servants in the employ of Sir Emmet

Harley, who, judging by the way in which they were both dressed, obviously thought very highly of them. Rosina Perez had originally been employed in Lima as maid to the late Lady Harley, and her brother, by a fortuitous coincidence, had worked as a manservant for one Robert Laurence, or Laurent, who, it would be shown to the court, had been working actively against British interests in South America.

During the past eighteen months, Rosina had picked up some English, and when she faltered, there was a Spanish interpreter to help both her and her brother through his own evidence. Rosina's story was carefully manufactured on a firm base of truth, so that it seemed much more believable than Anne's own version.

On the morning of the twentieth day of January, 1811, Sir Emmet and Lady Harley, accompanied by Sir Emmet's then ward, Miss Stacey, had been invited to attend a special thanksgiving service in the cathedral at Lima. This service was the preliminary to a fiesta in Lima, held to celebrate the miraculous rediscovery of a priceless set of statuettes known as the Golden Apostles. Whilst she was assisting Lady Harley with her toilette, a message had arrived for Rosina from her brother, which she immediately relayed to Lady Harley, who was greatly alarmed.

Francisco had just found out that his employer, the pleasant and dashing Mr. Robert Laurence, was in reality a French spy, and worse still, Miss Stacey intended eloping with him. Lady Harley went immediately to Miss Stacey's room, but she had already left with her own maidservant and confidante, Mrs. Waters. A quick search revealed that Miss Stacey had taken some light hand luggage. Then, despite Rosina's warnings, she decided to go, herself, to Robert Laurence's lodgings, which were but a few minutes' walk away, and endeavour to persuade Miss Stacey from her course.

Asked why Lady Harley had not gone straight to her husband, who, after all, was Miss Stacey's guardian, Rosina blinked her strange greenish eyes as if flicking away tears.

Lady Harley worried very much about Sir Emmet, who had been extremely fatigued owing to his affairs in Lima not going as well as he had hoped. Spanish America was difficult for an Englishman who did not understand its ways.

When Lady Harley, accompanied by Rosina, arrived at Robert Laurence's lodgings, there was a fearful scene, culminating when

Robert Laurence drew out his pistol and shot poor Lady Harley (here, Rosina crossed herself) through the heart, so that the poor lady fell straight to the floor dead. Then, despite her own efforts, and those of her brother Francisco, who had come running at the sound of the shot, Robert Laurence and Miss Stacey fled, accompanied by Mrs. Waters. This was the time when the pirates and bandits raided Lima, snatching away the precious Golden Apostles and other treasures, and such was the confusion, that it was quite an hour or more before she, Rosina, and her brother could fetch help.

'But it is all untrue!' protested Anne. 'Rosina was not there, and neither was her brother. Lady Harley was already dead. The old lady who owned the house, and her servant, both watched as Christie and myself were taken away by Robert Laurence and Captain Ducaine. Surely, when poor Inez's body was found, they told the authorities what had happened.'

Anne was back in her prison, and she paced back and forth with her skirt swishing about her ankles, barely able to control her anger.

Her barrister shook his head.

'Rest assured that I have studied the documents brought back from Lima by Sir

Emmet Harley. There is a report from the magistrate who investigated the murder, and I have had it translated. The old lady was almost blind. She could distinguish nothing but moving shapes. She was quite aware that something was very much amiss, but unable to give details. Her servant, who was seventy nine years of age, was so overcome by events that he collapsed from a heart seizure and died before he could be consulted.'

'Rosina is lying.' Anne frowned in concentration, reliving the scene as she had so often before. 'Lady Harley was on the floor, dead, when I and my servant arrived. Francisco could easily have killed her . . . or, Emmet.'

The last would explain the smart appearance of the pair. Sir Emmet Harley was paying them to repeat their preposterous lies. Yet, all the while, she felt that there was something she should have known, but could not reach. It was like a feather, or a wisp of thistledown in the breeze, floating out of reach as her fingers almost grasped it. On that day in Lima, she had seen, had noticed something, but the horrific events had blotted it out of her memory.

Then, she became very frightened, and her slim hands went up to her neck, as if guarding it against the strangling rope.

'Sir Emmet's secretary, Mr. Baxter,' she said. 'Surely he remembers that day.'

'That he does, but Mr. Baxter can tell us nothing except that he was closetted with Sir Emmet from eight in the morning until it was discovered that both yourself and Lady Harley were missing. No, Miss Stacey, I'm afraid that all evidence, yours included, points to the murder having been committed by Robert Laurence. However, the point at issue, I must remind you, is whether or not you were involved in a conspiracy with Robert Laurence.'

'I wasn't, and he didn't kill Lady Harley. In his own way, Mr. Laurence was an honourable man.'

Rosina had not finished. Lady Harley, she was glad to reply to questions, had confided in her that Miss Stacey was the cause of great anxiety to both Sir Emmet and his wife. Miss Stacey was very impressionable, and plainly charmed by the worldly Mr. Laurence.

This was flatly denied by Anne. She hesitated to cast shame upon a dead woman, but she declared emphatically that Lady Harley had actually been the one charmed by Mr. Laurence.

A document, dictated by Sir Emmet Harley from his sick bed, and duly witnessed by persons in good standing, was produced, in which he stated that Lady Harley had repeatedly told him that his ward, Anne Elizabeth Stacey, had formed an infatuation for Robert Laurence.

Lady Harley had done so, Anne thought bitterly, to draw attention away from her own interest in the planter.

'It must be remembered,' said the judge in his summing up, 'that the charge is not one of the murder of Lady Harley. That is a matter beyond the jurisdiction of this court, and documents from the relevant authorities in Lima leave no doubt that Lady Harley was killed by Robert Laurence, or Laurent, as he was also known. Robert Laurence is now himself dead, or so we have been led to believe by the defendant. The matter to be considered is whether or not Anne Elizabeth Stacey is guilty of the treasonable act of conspiring with the said Robert Laurence, or Laurent, to rob an allied power of a treasure which could have immeasurably helped the cause of Napoleon Bonaparte. On the other hand, it must be borne in mind that the defendant may well be of an impressionable and easily swayed nature.'

'No!'

Her voice screamed out in that crowded and stifling courtroom. Fans moving in the hands of the fashionable stopped dead.

'I am innocent! They are lying!' She pointed at Rosina and Francisco Perez, whose pale copper faces simultaneously reflected outraged surprise. Francisco actually rose to his feet in a movement of bemused indignation.

'Make them tell the truth! Bring Sir Emmet Harley here! Why isn't he here?'

At this point, she was hustled from the court to an anteroom, leaving behind an atmosphere shattered by sensation. After a few moments, she calmed herself sufficiently to listen to the barrister who had hurried after her.

He told her that he was confident that her sentence would be transportation. The judge, in his address, had hinted that justice should be tempered with mercy.

'Mercy! I'm innocent of what they say. And why are you so sure that the verdict must be guilty?'

He could not quite meet her eyes as she continued.

'Why won't they wait until Lucius Stanton is traced?'

He shrugged. He had taken off his wig, revealing his carefully cropped, slightly greying locks, and he now fanned himself with the peruke.

'My dear Miss Stacey, I am afraid that the

court is not prepared to await the testimony of convicted felons. The war has gone on too long, and too many people in this country are suffering because of it. They can wreak a little of their wrath upon you. I know that if I had been able to prove the existence of the men you describe, it would have gone in your favour, but quite obviously, they were both sheltering under false names, and the bench is not disposed to allow anything up to several years to elapse whilst they are traced. I'm sorry. I have done my best.'

'You think that I am guilty and that I will be sentenced, don't you?'

He waited a few seconds before replying.

'Unfortunately,' he said, wearily, 'I know that young women sometimes act very foolishly when in love. My instinct is that you are innocent of any treason, Miss Stacey, but I cannot fight solid testimony with instinct.'

She was found guilty by a jury which, however much it believed itself impartial, was worried by the burdens of war. There was a recommendation that the death sentence should not be imposed, and Anne was sentenced to seven years' exile in New South Wales.

Comfort of a sort was offered by the barrister, who seemed to think that he had done very well by her, all things considered.

'A boyhood friend of mine, poor old Harry Hayes of Cork, got himself mixed up in some stupid business over an abducted heiress, oh, ten years ago it must be. He certainly didn't need her money, because as soon as he arrived in Sydney, he arranged to buy a large estate just out of town. And there he has been, as comfortable as you like, ever since, acting the squire even though he's a felon. Please do not despair of your fate, Miss Stacey. Even when one is transported, one can pull strings if one has money, and I am sure you will be able to buy privileges.'

'I don't want privileges,' she snapped. 'I want justice.'

These were brave words which were not much comfort in the dark misery of night. Yet, she did sleep, and dreamt vividly that she was back in her cabin on board *The Eagle* as the vessel lay off the shore at Tahiti.

'Do not despair!'

The voice was so real that she was awakened, and lay, rigid, expecting to hear the splash of paddles in the water as she had on that night so many months earlier. Instead, she heard the sounds of Newgate at night, the whisperings, the rustlings, the footsteps, the clangings, the altercations in the wretched common apartments, a woman's shrill sobs, and a child crying out for its mother.

It was only a dream. There was no brave missionary here to give her heart when all seemed lost, and no brave young man known as Botany to pit his wits against all odds, and eventually carry her off to freedom.

16

She thought that they had come to move her to the convict transport in preparation for the long voyage to New South Wales, but instead, the turnkey let in Mr. Bretherton, the lawyer, the governor of Newgate, and, as an extra surprise, Major Anthony Bretherton who was leaning heavily on a cane, but otherwise appeared to be reasonably active.

They were all smiling, broadly, with not at all the looks of persons who had come to commiserate. Later, she remembered thinking, Tony looks much older, but in a thrice, everything was swept away in an incredible wave of joy.

She was free.

A document had arrived two days before, there had been a special hearing in a closed court, and it was ruled that in view of the new evidence, all charges against her had to be dismissed and her sentence nullified. They had not told her, they said, because they did not wish to raise her hopes.

'A miracle,' said Mr. Bretherton. 'We never lost faith, and now our prayers have been answered. I can tell you, m'dear, that all I want is to take this fellow Stanton by the hand and thank him from the bottom of my heart, all our hearts, as far as that goes.'

'Oh, you must use every means in your power to see that he is not punished further for escaping from New South Wales,' she cried. 'You see,' she continued, turning to the amused barrister, 'there *was* a Lucius Stanton. I cannot understand why you could not find his name.'

'I'm afraid,' was the dry reply, 'that we were looking in the wrong places. Mr. Stanton is a lieutenant in His Majesty's Royal Navy.'

★ ★ ★

The following is a statement made by Lieutenant P. Lucius Stanton, R.N., on the 2nd day of July, 1812.

'On the 10th of February, 1811, I was ordered to take my command, the sloop *Acmon* of His Majesty's Royal Navy, from Sydney, New South Wales, to Otahiete (or Tahiti, as it is also known) to investigate complaints that several escaped convicts from the New South Wales penal settlements had taken refuge there and were causing ill feeling between the natives and visiting Europeans.

'Unfortunately, *Acmon* was delayed on the

211

voyage by bad weather, and upon arrival, some small repairs were necessary. I also learned that the convicts in question had removed themselves by joining up as crew on some whaling ships which had recently called at the island.

'It was by now the end of April, and I was eager to be on our way back to Sydney before the deepening of the southern winter. However, I received a message from the Reverent Mr. Nott, the only remaining missionary on Tahiti, that there was at another anchorage some miles away an ostensibly American vessel which he strongly suspected of being a pirate. Mr. Nott, I must explain, after many difficult times, now enjoyed the confidence of King Pomare, ruler of Tahiti, whom he was teaching to read and write.

'The captain of this vessel, *The Eagle*, had with him on his visits ashore a female companion, a young English-woman, and as several Tahitian couples were about to be married and a large feast held for them, King Pomare suggested to this man, Captain Ducaine, that he should marry the young woman. Ducaine wished to ingratiate Pomare, as I later heard, so that he could take with him several natives to replace crew members lost in a violent storm. (Actually, some of these lost men had been killed during an unsuccessful mutiny.)

'The woman, Christie Waters, or Walters, I am not sure, confided to Mr. Nott that there was another young woman being held prisoner on *The Eagle*, both having been abducted during a pirate raid on Lima, in Peru. The other woman, also English, was said to be both wealthy and of high social standing.

'This placed me in a quandary, for observation revealed that *The Eagle* was a large brigantine, both heavier and faster than *Acmon*. Whether she carried much armament, it was impossible to ascertain from a distance, but she had definitely been built for speed, with little superstructure, in the manner favoured by some United States shipyards. She flew an American flag, and I was fully aware of difficulties which had already arisen through Royal Navy interception of American vessels.

'Foolishly, I realised too soon, I decided to reconnoitre, taking with me Able Seaman James Thomas, a youth of seventeen. I left *Acmon* under the command of my midshipman, and with both myself and Thomas disguised, we hoped, as escaped convicts from New South Wales, we boarded *The Eagle* under the pretext of wishing to trade. Unknown to myself, Ducaine had been refused by King Pomare in his request for crew members, and we were seized and locked below until *The Eagle* was well out to sea.

'When we were allowed on deck, I perceived the lady reputed to be a prisoner. She was plainly in a distressed state, having been confined in a small cabin during the whole stay at Tahiti, a time of over two weeks. She was badly dressed in a garment made from trade cotton, and barefoot. On deck, she was restricted to a small area, this being partly sheltered by an awning, and it was forbidden that members of the crew should address her. In truth, she had little desire to communicate with anyone on board, but I managed to exchange a few trivialities, and elicited from her mode of speech that she was indeed gently bred.

'The woman passing as Mrs. Ducaine — I soon heard in the focsle that Ducaine had a legal wife back in the United States — had been servant to Miss Anne Stacey, the prisoner, who in turn was ward of Sir Emmet Harley, a British envoy in South America. Mrs. Ducaine, so-called, apparently still had a kindness for her former mistress, for Ducaine was a man of uncertain temper, and she ran a considerable risk when she told

Mr. Nott of Miss Stacey's plight.

'Meanwhile, James Thomas and myself were in almost as difficult a situation as that of Miss Stacey, and we resolved to play out our parts as convicts who had escaped from Sydney, explaining our familiarity with seamen's work with a tale of having been employed on coastal shipping off New South Wales. We did not ask too many questions, but kept our ears open, and soon affirmed Mr. Nott's suspicion, that *The Eagle* was a common pirate. Actually, the brigantine belonged to a respectable New England merchant, who, in good faith, had despatched Ducaine to Vancouver Island to trade for sea otter skins, which in turn were to be traded in China. Ducaine had been engaged in such enterprises before, but he had formed a desire to assist Bonaparte in any way he could, and at the same time, advance his own fortunes. Of French descent, he carried a grudge against England far greater, I believe, than that of most Frenchmen actually engaged in warfare against us. As crew he had gathered together a pack of sea rats, of many nationalities owing allegiance to no country, and began raiding the Pacific ports of New Spain. At first, his success was only moderate, for *The Eagle* carried little heavy armament, and he had to rely on quick surprise raids.

'By a stroke of luck, whilst trying to spy out the lie of the land at a small port in northern Peru, Ducaine met Robert Laurence, a former acquaintance also known as Laurent, a French agent who was trying to foster a revolution in Peru. Laurence told Ducaine of an enormously valuable treasure which had been lost for centuries, and having been recently recovered, was being transported from the mountains to Lima. Laurence had gathered together a band of Indian and mestizo revolutionaries with the intention of seizing this treasure to finance his plans, and Ducaine offered to help him. Together, the two parties successfully carried off the treasure, known as the Golden Apostles, but Ducaine had no intention that this wealth should be used in Peru. He had dreams of rising high in Bonaparte's favour, and he betrayed Laurence's followers by taking the treasure to *The Eagle* and immediately setting sail. Virtually by accident, the two young women were abducted, for Ducaine immediately saw the value of Miss Stacey as a hostage if it became necessary to save his own skin. He also took with him the spy Laurence, who was badly wounded, because Ducaine, raised in New England, had little knowledge of the French tongue and foresaw Laurence's usefulness as an interpreter.

'In fact, Laurence died before *The Eagle* reached Tahiti, while helping Ducaine quell a mutiny by some of the crew. At this time, most of the crew still had faith in their captain, believing that he intended finding a desert island suitable for the purpose of melting down the Apostles so that the gold could be fairly divided. Incidentally, it was from Miss Stacey that I gained the information that Laurence was to have been an interpreter, and at my suggestion, she managed to pass on, through her former servant, that I had some knowledge of the French language. (There were two Frenchmen on board, but they were Bretons who spoke only their own language.)

'There was also on board a mulatto called Daniel, believed by the crew to possess the Evil Eye, and there had apparently been a long association between this person and Ducaine, so much so that when Daniel accidentally died on an island at which we called to take on fresh water, Ducaine appeared to lose some of his former confidence. By this time, the crew were becoming openly dissatisfied about Ducaine's plans, which attitude I did my humble best to foster. By now, I was sure that our destination was Java, and I warned Miss Stacey, still not revealing my true calling for I feared that if my deception and that of James Thomas were discovered things could go badly with her, that I would attempt to escape when the time was right.

'All this while, Miss Stacey had acted with great dignity, and never once yielded in any way, although her position, with her former servant now privileged as captain's wife, was extremely difficult and lonely. Some of the men developed tropical ulcers, James Thomas amongst them, and Mrs. Ducaine, so called, refused to treat them, and Miss Stacey undertook this repugnant task. It gave me the opportunity to communicate with her, and as well, earned her considerable respect and liking amidst even the hardened ruffians of *The Eagle*'s crew. This worked to our advantage as will be seen.

'As we approached the coast of Java, I resolved that I must endeavour to reach Penang. I also felt that it was my duty to hinder Ducaine in any way possible, and James Thomas and myself managed to stove in a couple of planks below the waterline. Ducaine's goal was Batavia, where, I gathered, he had a proposition to lay before the governor, but now he was forced to call in at a small harbour on the northern coast of the eastern part of Java.

'Here, during conversation with two French

officers, I at last learnt the true purpose of Ducaine's voyage. One of the Frenchmen had spent time in India during his youth, and Ducaine's interest in this fact — remembering that the Frenchmen had absolutely no idea that such wealth was carried on *The Eagle* — convinced me that his purpose was not to use the gold to consolidate the French position in the East Indies, but to actually bribe certain dissident Indian princes into rebellion against the British.

'As a naval officer, it had become imperative that I must reach the British station at Penang, and I determined to seize a little yacht owned by the French commandant, this craft being rather larger than a skiff but not so big as a pinnace, and easily managed by two men. Miss Stacey, I was resolved, should come with us. For some time, there had been rumours on board that Ducaine might sell her into slavery, and now the captain made arrangements that the French officers would take her in order to hold her to ransom, this being payment for the supplies he needed. The crew protested at this plan, for they held Miss Stacey in high regard, and wished that she be transferred to one of the British ships blockading Java so that she could return to her own people. They also realised that they would receive very little of the booty gathered during their raids.

'Led by the mate, they made Ducaine a prisoner, and prepared to leave for a destination of their own choosing. At this time, the two French officers I mentioned earlier came on board, and were taken prisoner. Able Seaman Thomas, of whom I cannot speak too highly, for his courage never faltered, and despite his youth, he carried himself like a veteran of Nelson's greatest battles, now carried out our pre-arranged plan and set fire to *The Eagle*. In the panic he, myself, and Miss Stacey made our escape.

'Miss Stacey, unhappily, had yielded to a tropical fever, and our voyage was of such difficulty that I cast aside my idea of trying to reach Penang, and instead set sail for Batavia in the hope that there she could be nursed back to health. I was in the greatest despair, for the winds were unfavourable, but when all seemed lost, God heard my prayers and those of James Thomas, and delivered us safely into the hands of our countrymen. As all are now aware, a great fleet, with Lord Minto, the Governor-General of India, in command, sailed successfully against the prevailing winds of that season to attack and take Java.

'Miss Stacey was placed immediately on

board a despatch vessel sailing back to Malacca. She was unaware of what was happening, and it was with heavy hearts that we both parted with her, for we feared that this brave young lady would not survive.

'To learn that this young lady, who had suffered so much, was charged with treason caused me much shock and anger. She was a victim of cruel circumstances, and although her servant, Christie Waters, was happy to better her position with the scoundrel Ducaine, Miss Stacey, I am convinced, never budged in her loyalty to her country.'

★ ★ ★

Anne did not see this document, but she was told enough of its contents to grasp several facts. By far and away the most important was that she had been right in her instinct to trust Lucius Stanton. He had been worthy of her faith, and he had told her his true name. At the same time, she felt that she had misjudged Christie in that however reprehensible the servant's behaviour had been, she had retained enough conscience to tell Mr. Nott, the missionary, of her mistress's plight, perhaps in the slight hope that he would prevail upon Ducaine to set Anne free in Tahiti. Mr. Nott, of course, had done what would seem right and rational to a British subject — he had informed a British naval officer.

She asked whether Lieutenant Stanton was in London, but no one knew. As days passed, it seemed that Lucius Stanton, having done his duty, was not of a mind to renew their acquaintanceship.

During her trial, she had thought that freedom would solve every problem, but instead, it brought with it a fresh crop of complications and worries. She had been saved from punishment for a crime of which she was not guilty, but her life had been changed forever. She was no longer a circumspect heiress under the protection of a stern guardian, but a woman who had attained notoriety through being captured by pirates and living as their prisoner for several months. As well, the mystery surrounding Lady Harley's death still remained as a question mark over her good name.

Tony Bretherton was all for going immediately to Whitestairs and insisting, at the point of his sword if necessary, that Sir Emmet clear her of the lingering suspicion that she had been involved in his wife's murder.

'There has been enough scandal already,' she told the impetuous major, but already, the elation attending her freedom was subsiding.

'It's as plain as the nose on your face that those Indians murdered Lady Harley,' retorted Tony. 'And I'll lay that Sir Emmet put them up to it. That's the only explanation!'

Neither was Mr. Bretherton going to permit matters to rest, although he was less impetuous about it than his son. He was insisting that the activities of Rosina Perez and her rascally brother should be thoroughly investigated.

'The law's too slow,' snapped the major. 'Once they get wind of the Runners, they'll be into hiding, with Emmet's connivance to boot. I wonder how much he inherited from Inez!'

One part of Anne wished to bring it all to a head, the other wished for a time of quiet, of isolation, whilst her spirits mended. Somewhat to her surprise, the old family solicitor whom she had consulted about a residence for herself had carried out her instructions, and now she had a list to study and assess. It gave her something to do, helping dull the disappointment she felt because Lucius Stanton had not called upon her, nor made any attempt to communicate directly with her.

During those days of reorientation, she and Major Bretherton discussed their relationship. To her enormous relief, he did not utter any protestations, but rather, was happy to resume the cousinly affection which had existed between them since childhood.

'The way in which your father and my aunt retained their faith in me was of the greatest comfort, Tony, and I am so sorry that I no longer feel that I can marry you.'

Major Bretherton was seated opposite her, on a most uncomfortable chair which had been inspired by the temple drawings of Ancient Egypt. It was not long enough to be a bench, and a little too broad for a stool. This whole drawingroom had been decorated in the antiquarian style inspired by Napoleon's sojourn in Egypt. This craze had briefly swept the salons of Western Europe and Britain, but now, blessedly, was going out of fashion, for the ancients had apparently been impervious to the need for furniture to conform to human contours.

'Ah, Anne, we've both changed, so much.'

He was usually such a cheerful young man, but as he spoke, he was uncharacteristically solemn.

'I began to doubt before my terrible adventures,' she said, trying to subdue the lump in her throat. 'You must think me a fickle, foolish miss.'

'No, m'dear. We've both grown up. There've been times over the past two years when I've felt a thousand years old. So many brave fellows dead, and so much suffering which need not have been if the government here at Home weren't so stingy. Trouble is, people don't want to hear about the war as it is. They're quick enough to go wild over victories, but it isn't fashionable to dwell on the wounded, and the lack of supplies, and the whole confounded wretchedness. Now the Monster's into Russia. When is it going to end, Anne? It's been going on since we were both children.'

She had never heard him speak in such a serious vein before, and she felt a great sorrow that she would not marry this man. For a few moments, they both sat quietly, and then he grinned, returning to the happy-go-lucky Tony she knew so well.

'That isn't the sort of talk a young lady wants to hear. I think I'll hobble round to my club. I don't much like being a cripple, but at least, I'm alive.'

The whole household was by now preparing for its return to the country, and for Anne's part, she was very glad. London was intolerably hot and noisy, and most of society had already fled, a circumstance for which she was glad. She was of too proud and refined a nature to wish for the sort of publicity which had followed her trial. Some, she knew, appeared to thrive upon notoriety, but the glances which followed her on the few occasions she dared go abroad made her feel that she had become a freak.

There was something which she had almost forgotten in the midst of her troubles, and that was the return of her jewellery which had remained in Sir Emmet Harley's possession. She decided to take matters into her own hands by composing a letter to the baronet.

Once she had the quill in her hand, this task became very difficult. When she had first made up her mind, the words had flowed in her mind. Now, they dried on her pen. Dear Sir Emmet. Dear Emmet. Oh, how did one address the villain? Sir? Just Sir? Sir, I wish to draw your attention to the matter of my jewellery which has not been returned to me. Ah, that was better.

She began spreading the words in neat lines across the paper, and then inspiration failed again.

There was a discreet tap on the door.

A Mr. Lucius Stanton was below, wishing the pleasure of a few words with Miss Stacey.

Her aunt had gone out for a last visit

to London's shops. The young girls, her cousins, were out walking demurely with their governess. The house was in an upheaval of packing. Where to receive him? The morning room was half dust-sheeted. It would have to be the drawingroom with its absurd furniture and improbable wallpaper illustrated with jerky little Egyptian figures and imitation hieroglyphics.

How did she look? Not quite as she would have wished, for she was wearing a plain gown and her hair was pulled into a simple knot on the crown. But there was no time to change. All the dreariness and despondency of the past days had gone, and she hurried down to see the man who had been so often in her dreams and secret longings.

17

He took her hand, formally, and wished that she was well.

In his rough dress on board *The Eagle*, he had been lithe and free in his movements. In what was obviously a brand new set of clothes, he was stiff and constrained.

'How can I ever thank you,' she said, in a low and fervent voice. 'You have done so much for me. I owe you more than words can tell, and I had feared so much that I would not have the opportunity to see you and speak with you.'

'I shall be leaving this country very soon,' he replied, quite abruptly. 'we are now at war with the United States, as you must be aware, and I'm bound for American waters.'

As he spoke, his lean brown features became even sterner.

'Miss Stacey, if I could beg a few minutes of your time, I shall explain the reason for my call.'

Does there have to be a reason, she cried out silently. She was hurt and puzzled. They had been through so much together, and there seemed to be but one explanation for his indifference. He was married.

'Mr. Stanton, I do hope that before you offer explanations, you will tell me what happened after we were separated,' she said, crisply.

Then she suggested that they both seat themselves, but he declined her offer of refreshment. After a somewhat dubious glance about himself, he chose a solidly square chair with lion's feet. If Anne had not been so upset, she would have noticed that he had picked a position from which he could obtain the most flattering view of herself.

'After we parted,' he said, 'I had to answer a great many questions from the officers commanding the expedition to capture Java, and eventually, I was despatched on a ship carrying a well-armed contingent of Indian troops in the hope of finding *The Eagle*'s crew on the coast near where we had left her. We did find *The Eagle* lying on her side in shallow water, half burnt out, and deserted by her crew. Before they left, they'd shot Ducaine and strung him up on what was left of the foremast.'

Anne's right hand went to her lips. She had hated and feared Ducaine, but she was still shocked at the summary way in which he had been executed by his own crew.

'And Christie?'

This mattered very much to her. Christie had been responsible for bringing on board the two young men who had dared so much on her behalf, and whatever else she had done, Anne now felt nothing but gratitude towards her erstwhile servant.

'The two Frenchmen took her with them when they escaped,' he explained, pausing, and for the first time smiling in that attractive, rather carefree way she remembered so vividly. 'I did not enlarge too much upon Mrs. Waters. The last I heard, she was personal maid to the wife of one of the British administrators in Java.'

'I'm glad. She was foolish, and at times quite horrid, but I wish her no ill. Poor Christie! She thought that she was going to become enormously rich. Mr. Stanton, after my own experiences, I think I can understand a little how it feels to be poor and without privilege.'

There was a brief silence, which she broke by asking whether the treasure had been recovered. The Apostles, after all, had been the major cause of her troubles.

'In a manner of speaking, yes,' he answered, somewhat mysteriously. 'I must

230

admit that I puzzled often over the whereabouts of their hiding place, as did every other
member of the crew, but Mistress Christie
was either privy to Ducaine's deepest secrets,
or she was smarter than we suspected and was
able to work out where the statuettes were
concealed. After the wreck keeled over — and
remember, Miss Stacey, that *The Eagle* was
taking in water which prevented her being
completely destroyed by the fire — Mrs.
Waters indicated to her French friends the
position of the treasure, and after some
difficulty, a great shapeless mess of gold was
recovered. Gold is a soft metal, Miss Stacey,
and the heat of the fire was sufficient to ruin
the statuettes before the vessel became partly
submerged. What became of the other loot
on board, I do not know. Perhaps our pirate
friends managed to retrieve it to help them on
their way, or perhaps it is somewhere deep in
the wreck on the ocean bed.'

She knew that he was teasing her a little
by not telling her the exact location of the
statuettes' hiding place, but the information,
uttered with a small, wry smile, caused her
to gasp.

'I don't believe it! I was sleeping over the
Golden Apostles!'

It was incredible, but he assured her that
was the truth. Daniel, the dead mulatto, had

constructed the extra bunk in the cabin which was to accommodate the female prisoners. This bunk, she knew, had been nothing but a crude inverted box, with no locker space beneath. From the first, she had chosen the makeshift bunk because it was directly under the porthole, and as mistress, it had seemed only proper that she should have the extra comfort of a breeze on hot nights. So much was now explained, She had not only been a hostage, but guardian of the treasure, which was why she had been securely locked in her cabin whilst *The Eagle* had called at Tahiti!

After these explanations, there was one more thing to be told, and that, at last, was the real reason for Stanton's visit. James Thomas, Jemmy, had died of fever a few days after the recovery of the gold which had been the Apostles.

She felt the rush of tears to her eyes.

'Oh, I am so sorry. He was such a fine boy.'

'Yes. Miss Stacey, can you help his family? His mother is a widow now, and like so many of our poorer folk, she is having a desperately hard time of it. There are younger children, and the poor good soul has a dread of their all being thrown upon the parish. She does her best to support them as a laundress, but as they grow, so do their appetites. There is a lad of an age to be apprenticed, but his mother cannot afford it. He fancies printing. And there is a girl just twelve years old. She seems a well-behaved, industrious little thing, and perhaps you could find her a place in a decent household.'

He did not pretend to be other than imploring her, and she nodded quickly, hardly trusting herself to speak.

'I'll make no bones about it, Miss Stacey — since my return, I've been shocked to see how much poorer the poor have become. The well-to-do weep over the fate of poor black slaves, but ignore the suffering which is on their own doorstep.'

The words echoed in her mind, and she stared at him.

'What a strange thing to say,' she announced.

'Strange?' His manner once again became very stiff and formal. 'And why should that be strange?'

'Because,' she said, slowly and deliberately, 'that is exactly what Robert Laurence said to me a short time before he died.'

An awkward silence fell between them. She was bitterly disappointed: all the dreams she had built up about this man went crashing to the ground. When she had learned that he was not a convict, but a respectable naval officer, it seemed that prayers had been answered. Now he was so remote in his manner that she hardly knew what to say, and what really stung was that the true reason why he had called was to beg her help for poor Jemmy's family.

'I shall do all I can for Mrs. Thomas and her family,' she promised, rising, so that this uncomfortable interlude could come to an end. 'You must give me all the details of her whereabouts.'

As she spoke, she felt utterly wretched. She wanted so badly to have this man show again some of the tenderness towards her he had displayed during those half-remembered days when she had been so sick with fever.

It was at this moment, when she thought that they were about to part forever, that Major Bretherton burst into the room.

'They told me you'd come to call on my cousin! My dear fellow!' He hobbled across the room, hand out-stretched, his pleasant face beaming. 'I can imagine no one I'd rather meet!'

Anne hastily introduced them, and there sprung up almost immediately that special rapport which exists between men in the service of their country. So Stanton was off to American waters? Boney must be turning hand-springs in sheer delight at the knowledge that Britain's strength was being sapped by a war on another front.

'I don't mind the prospect of some action,' admitted Lucius Stanton, now much more at his ease. 'Being based in Sydney was not very exciting, I can tell you.'

'Though you had your share in the end, eh?' laughed Bretherton. 'I expect you know that our poor Anne is still having a bad time of it,' he continued, in a graver tone, and proceeded to tell the visitor that although she had been cleared of the treason charge, her good name must remain in doubt until Sir Emmet Harley issued a statement putting things to rights.

'If it weren't for this plaguey leg o' mine,' went on the major, vehemently, 'I'd call the scoundrel out. He put those servants up to it, there's no doubt of it at all, and he isn't man enough to come out into the open.'

Seeing Stanton's blank expression, he filled in details with his usual gusto, whilst Anne gently protested that the law would take its course and Rosina and Francisco would be charged with perjury.

'And how long is that going to take? No, Anne, we must have it out with him!'

Perhaps it was the wine which Major Bretherton poured and handed about, or perhaps it was that two young men of lively and adventurous dispositions were already bored by being away from active service.

'No!' said Anne, as their plans were formulated.

'It is no more than five miles out of my way on the road to Portsmouth where I am to join my ship,' insisted Lucius Stanton, and he thumped his fist on the mock-Egyptian wine table, threatening to split the gilded wood. 'I'd thought everything to be cleared up by my story of what happened on board *The Eagle*, and I'm going to see it all put to rights before I leave England. Miss Stacey, you have endured too much!'

'Good man!' enthused Major Bretherton. 'We'll beard Sir Emmet in his evil den, and get to the bottom of this business for once and for all!'

There were dismayed wails from her aunt. Surely Anne could wait until they all journeyed back to Hampshire. A day or two would not make much difference, and think of the talk which would be caused if she travelled in the company of two young men.

'Talk!' said her niece, mirthlessly. 'There is so much talk about me that little more can be said. In any case I have the addresses of two houses I wish to inspect, for you know it is my intention to set up an establishment of my own. And with Miss Howard to act as duenna, I am sure proprieties will be observed.'

Miss Howard was her new personal maid, a stern-faced person of forty impeccable summers. It was just as well that Miss Howard was kept in innocence of the true purpose of this journey into the countryside.

18

The weather was glorious, with the sunshine warming the fields of ripening corn, so that the countryside's poorer inhabitants could briefly forget last winter's miseries. Warm days helped counteract the hardship caused by the ever-spiralling cost of bread, and if the children outside the labourer's cottages seemed thinner than Anne remembered, at least they were happy enough to wave at the smart carriage as it rolled along its well-sprung way.

'My people had land here once,' said Stanton suddenly. 'They sold out twenty years ago. They couldn't compete against the big landholders.'

She glanced at him, understanding him a little better, and for the first time, it came to her that his diffidence could well be because of the difference in their wealth. It had not mattered when they were both captive on board *The Eagle*, but here in England, it was very important. He was no fortune-chaser. He was too brave and honourable a man for that, and but for the need to ask a favour for Jemmy Thomas's destitute family, perhaps she would never have seen him again. Now he was one of their little party, for two reasons. One, to share in this last episode of the story which had started with the theft of the Golden Apostles, and two, to be carried part of the way to Portsmouth in rather more style than he could have afforded on his frugal lieutenant's pay.

Even as she realised that the difference in their worldly status could be responsible for his formal manner when addressing her, common sense told her sternly that she had most likely mistaken his courage and kindness for something else. It was so hard to forget the time when he had held her hands, and looked into her eyes and told her to remember his name. Equally impossible was to obliterate all recollection of lying desperately ill in a small boat, when he had bathed her forehead, held a beaker to her dried and chapped lips and begged her not to die.

'We're nearly there!' said Major Bretherton at that moment.

Sir Emmet Harley had inherited White-stairs from his father, who had hired the best architect, the best builder and the most skilled decorator to design, erect and adorn the great mansion, set on a rise behind the magnificent terrace reached by the wide white steps which had given the house its name. Every artifice of the landscaper's art had turned ordinary land into scenery of constantly unfolding delight. Sir Emmet's father had been acquainted with Sir Joseph Banks, and the famed botanist-explorer had assisted in the choice of rare trees and shrubs, so that during a stroll through the park, one could wonder at specimens from all the continents of the world. Yet, not only scientific curiosity was satisfied. At every turn, there was something to please both eye and soul.

All this beauty and magnificence had come from sugar, a fact which Sir Emmet preferred to have forgotten now that slave-owning was considered obnoxious.

At the lodge, the old gatekeeper whom Anne remembered from former times came outside, and gaped when he realised that she was a passenger in the carriage.

'Miss Anne!' he exclaimed, and hurried forward, smiling and yet uneasy. 'I didn't expect to see you here!'

'I've business with Sir Emmet,' she replied, smiling in return. 'Are you well?'

Now he assumed a gloomy expression.

'Things aren't what they were, Miss Anne,' he said, shaking his head. 'It's not my place to speak — and oh, Major Bretherton!' He seemed absolutely overwhelmed but still, at the same time, worried. 'I heard in the village that you were back, sir. Miss Anne, I don't think Sir Emmet will see you, and that's the truth, and I'm surprised you want to see him.'

'That's our affair,' called out Tony Bretherton, but so jovially that no offence could be taken. 'Now open the gates for us, there's a good fellow.'

The old man still hesitated.

'There's strange things going on at the house,' he said, lowering his voice as if expecting to be overheard by those who could do him harm. 'You'll find it all very changed. Those who'd been with the family since the old baronet's time turned out and the whole house running to rack and ruin and those two Indians struttin' about like cocks o' the walk.'

The two young men exchanged significant glances, and Miss Howard, squeezed into her corner and still showing her disapproval of the whole mad venture, said something about consulting Mr. Bretherton senior before trespassing.

'Oh no,' said Major Bretherton. 'We're here and in we go. Take 'em by surprise, that's the drill, eh, Stanton?'

241

'That is the drill,' supported Stanton, with that flash of a smile which always had such a weakening effect upon Anne.

The gatekeeper decided to join in the conspiracy, and grinned momentarily.

'But perhaps Miss Anne should stay here?' he suggested. 'What's going on isn't right, and I'm telling you straight, Sir Emmet won't see you. He sees no one these days, or I reckon it's those two who won't let him be seen.'

'When did you see him last?' Tony Bretherton came straight to the point, for he was never one to go the long way round when a direct approach would work better.

'While that pair were up in London, sir, I kept an eye on Sir Emmet. Very poorly, he was. Mr. Bretherton, your father, sir, came calling, but Sir Emmet refused to see him.'

'You kept an eye on Sir Emmet!' Now it was Anne's turn. The mystery grew by the instant. 'Why yourself? I can't believe that all the servants are gone. And what about Sir Emmet's valet, Mr. Barnes?'

'All gone,' said the man, lugubriously. 'Even Mr. Barnes what had been with Sir Emmet since he was a lad.'

'Open those gates,' ordered Anne imperiously. 'We are going to see all this for ourselves.'

The long treelined avenue was as she

recalled, but already, there were the signs of neglect. A branch had fallen across the drive, and had to be removed by the coachman and the groom. The smooth sward of memory was overgrown, eaten down in places by the ornamental deer, or the horses which now roamed at will, unstabled and unkempt. The gravel near the house was unweeded and unraked during this summer at least. The neglect was still not great, but growing daily. Dead leaves and animal droppings lay on the broad white steps leading up to the terrace, and several domestic hens fluttered away as the carriage was pulled to a halt.

Anne alighted, assisted by Lucius Stanton, and joined by Major Bretherton, the trio stared up at the house. Most of the deepset windows were blank with drawn curtains, and despite the bright sun of high summer, there was an air of dark melancholy which made Anne shudder.

Resolutely, they went up the steps, and then marched across the terrace, Major Bretherton finding the bell pull in a niche near the main door and tugging at it briskly. Somewhere in the big house there was a responsive peal and a slamming door. Then there was a silence broken only by the cooing of pigeons high up under the roof.

This had always been an austere house,

243

splendidly kept, but without the warmth Anne had associated with her own home during her childhood. Today, and perhaps it was only imagination, she could sense fear. Instinctively she stepped closer to Lucius Stanton, and at that moment, Tony turned his head slightly and in his unguarded eyes, she saw the hurt. He still loved her, and she realised that he had spoken to her as he had, of growing up and changing, to make things easier for her.

He knew now where her love was directed, without understanding the hopelessness of it all. Lucius had risked his life to help her, as he would have risked his life for anyone in the same dreadful situation. On board *The Eagle*, he had held her hands and begged her to trust him because it was necessary for them both. He had not begged her to love him.

'No one will answer,' said Tony, in a disgusted voice, after some moments had elapsed, and the two young men sought about for another means of entry.

'There are other doors,' pointed out Anne, and the groom and coachman were enlisted to search these out, whilst Miss Howard remained in her seat, disapproving but bursting with curiosity.

Those within the house had anticipated

244

that other means of entry would be sought, and every entrance was discovered to be securely bolted against intruders.

'Nothing for it but a window,' said Lucius Stanton, and laughed. 'I've only just been cleared in an enquiry by my superiors as to exactly why I left my command in the middle of the Pacific Ocean. I wonder what will happen if I'm caught in the act of breaking and entering?'

This was the first Anne had heard of the enquiry. It had never even occurred to her that he would receive anything but praise for his efforts in forestalling Ducaine's attempt to supply the French with an invaluable aid to their plans in the East.

'No time to be thinking of if's and maybe's,' stated Major Bretherton. 'Stand clear, everyone.'

They all obeyed, and taking off his coat, he wrapped his left arm in it before smashing through the lower pane of one the tall windows looking out across the terrace over the shaggy lawns to the artificial lake sheltered by a grove of trees. After knocking out a few jagged shards of glass, he reached inside and unlocked the sash, pushing it up so that they could all step over the low sill and enter the house.

This was, Anne knew, a morning room, a

favourite of Inez's, less formal than the other rooms on the ground floor. The first thing she noticed was that it was filthy.

'Good lord,' breathed Stanton. 'This makes the Augean stables seem sweet by comparison.'

There were empty wine bottles on the tables, on shelves, and on the floor. Scraps of mouldering food on unwashed plates made a feast for flies. Expensive ornaments had been knocked over and lay broken on the soiled carpet. And the room stank.

Grimacing his repugnance, Bretherton called out to the coachman and groom to remain outside unless summoned, and the trio moved out into the great entrance hall. Here, everything was dusty and unswept, and a mouse scurried back to its hole.

Anne tried to hold her breath as she ran to the front door and undid the bolts, flinging it wide open so that the good fresh air and the afternoon sun rushed in to that dark and sorrowful house.

Above them, somewhere on the next floor, there was a rustling, like a woman's stiff silk dress, followed by a quick, sibilant whisper.

'Stand in a doorway, Anne,' said Tony, very quietly, and despite his limp, he began edging up the stairs, close to the wall, pistol

246

in hand. This weapon was one of a pair he had brought with him, normally used for target practice, and Stanton held the other, covering Bretherton as he moved up stair by stair.

'Stop!'

The voice was male and gutteral and that of a foreigner with little English. The stocky and swarthy Francisco Perez was at the top of the fine and sweeping staircase, holding a fowling piece. His sister was slightly to his rear.

'Go away!' she screamed. 'Sir Emmet 'Arley eez seek. You frighten 'eem.'

'I demand to see him,' said Anne, in a clear and carrying voice. 'I am his closest living relative and I have matters to discuss with him.'

'He won't see you. You . . . you . . . keeled Senora Inez.'

Tony interrupted with a few short sentences of frightfully mispronounced Spanish. It caught the Perez pair by surprise, as it did Anne, who understood enough to realise that this was the language of soldiery arguing with the obdurate or downright hostile. They were, said Tony, to cut out this infernal nonsense. Miss Stacey intended to see Sir Emmet Harley, who had done her a fearful wrong, and if they said again that she had killed

247

Senora Inez, he would personally arrange for the slow and painful removal of their tongues.

Inez recovered more quickly than her brother, who appeared to be somewhat dullwitted, for he stood stock still and blankfaced. She moved forward and screeched at Major Bretherton. It was a poor strategy, for she had broken the brief impasse of Bretherton pointing his pistol at Francisco who in his turn was aiming back with the fowling piece.

'Put down that gun!' said Lucius Stanton quietly, moving up the stairs quite openly, his pistol steady over his left forearm and Francisco in his sights.

Bretherton repeated the order in Spanish, and after an imploring glance at his sister, who was plainly the one who did all the thinking, the Peruvian obeyed.

This was by no means the end of the drama, for at this moment there marched through the front door two new arrivals on the scene, one of whom Anne recognised instantly. It was the same Runner who had come to the Bretherton's house with the warrant for her arrest.

'High time you arrived,' said Major Bretherton cheerfully as they tramped up the stairs to seize the pair and hustle them

248

down to the ground floor.

Lucius Stanton came to Anne, and smiled down at her.

'Major Bretherton and myself joined forces with the Runners,' he explained. 'We offered to find a way in if they backed us up.'

Anne scarcely heard him, for she was staring at the earrings and necklace Rosina wore. They were her own, part of her inheritance, the same jewels over which she had argued with Inez in faraway Lima. Then it all came into place, the floating, ungraspable something she could not quite remember of that morning when the great bells had pealed out joyously for the Golden Apostles, and she had stared in horror at Inez's lifeless body. Inez had not been wearing any jewellery. Even her small soft hands had been quite bare of rings. Inez had been killed for her jewellery.

'Our warrant is only for perjury,' said the senior of the two Runners, kindly, as she tried to explain to him, but Major Bretherton launched into his execrable though fluent Spanish, and Francisco crossed himself and cried out for mercy.

She had made him do it. She had told him that Lady 'Arley was running away from Sir Emmet, and that she would have jewellery with her. Rosina arrived with her mistress too early for the Senor Laurence, and when they tried to pull off her rings and earrings and necklace, the woman had screamed and they were frightened someone would catch them and he took Senor Laurence's pistol which Senor Laurence had given him in case he had to protect the Lady 'Arley, and shot her dead.

What to do? Rosina had always possessed a cool head. Make it all appear different, she said, as if Senor Laurence had killed the Lady 'Arley because she had caught the golden haired one running away with the Americano. No one had seen Rosina and her mistress leaving the Harley house, so Rosina slipped back to entice the Senorita into the trap. The confusion following the raid helped. There was no Senorita Stacey to deny everything, and the stolen jewellery was replaced on Inez's body, so that it looked exactly as Rosina said. They had all thought that Senorita Stacey was dead, but she came back.

Major Bretherton translated this, and the senior of the Runners said, 'Well, well, well,' and whistled silently.

'All we need now,' said Lucius Stanton, 'is to find Sir Emmet and have it out with him too.'

Most of the vast house was closed off, with

only a very few rooms, all filthy, having been in use recently. Sir Emmet Harley was in none of these.

As they went from door to door, opening them and peering inside each unused room, Lucius Stanton explained how he and Major Bretherton had put their heads together. Tony had located Mr. Baxter, now with a new employer. The baronet's former secretary had at first been unwilling to discuss Sir Emmet, for he had been happy in Harley's employ for several years. However, even the discreet Mr. Baxter found it hard to keep bottled up his anger and resentment at his treatment, which was mixed with some genuine concern for Sir Emmet. His former employer's behaviour had become increasingly erratic in the weeks which followed Lady Harley's death, so much so that the British ambassador in Peru had sent him back to England. Within a week of their arrival, Baxter was dismissed without explanation, although Baxter was sure that it was at the suggestion of Rosina Perez, who now ran the whole household. He was quite sure that Sir Emmet would not have attempted to have his ward, Miss Stacey, convicted of treason had he been in his right mind. According to Mr. Baxter, Sir Emmet was, in his own way, fond of his young relative, and although he had been both angry and distressed at her involvement with Mr. Laurence who had turned out to be a French agent, it seemed very strange that a man with so much family pride would draw attention to such a scandal by accusing the young lady of treason.

The coachman, groom, and the still disapproving Miss Howard now joined the search, and they divided this huge house into sections, each to be thoroughly examined.

'Oh, dear God,' said Anne wearily, 'have they killed him?'

An hour later, with the Runners still keeping their prisoners under close guard, the searchers met again in the entrance hall, baffled and frightened.

'What have you done with him?' Anne demanded of the Perez brother and sister, who sat, sullen-faced and yet strangely smug. Rosina's green eyes were like glass set in a carving of an Inca face. Torture would not crack her now.

The stables and outhouses were searched next, still without result.

'They couldn't have had time to have moved him far,' said Bretherton gloomily. 'Always supposing that he did not hurry off somewhere himself rather than face you, Anne.'

'It reminds me of the Apostles,' said

252

Stanton, slowly. 'They were hidden in such an obvious place.'

Of course!

'Come with me,' she ordered, and ran up the splendid staircase and along the main first floor corridor leading to the south wing. Here the corridor ended in a panelled wall with a window set high.

'I should have remembered this,' she said. 'That is not a true window. The light is reflected from a light well. If only I can find it. Sir Emmet's father showed it to me years ago, when I was a small child.'

'Do you mean to say that there's a secret room in there? Dash it all, Anne, this is not a house in a Gothic tale. It's no more than twenty five years old,' expostulated Major Bretherton who was becoming extremely impatient.

'When it was built,' explained Anne, 'Sir Emmet's father had an elderly aunt who was quite eccentric, poor soul, with a great fear of other people and open spaces. She lived in a small suite of rooms behind that wall, with a private staircase going down to the conservatory where there is another hidden door. If only I can remember, oh, which is it, the third panel from the right, or the fourth?'

Her fingers flew over the carving, pressing

and feeling, until there was a click as the beautifully concealed door swung inwards.

The apartment was cobwebbed from long disuse, and there on a dust-sheeted chair sat Emmet Harley, thin and hollow-faced, a man in another world, lost in dreams, the poor drugged puppet who for months had been both victim and tool of Rosina Perez.

19

Anne sat at her writing desk. Outside, the first gales of autumn rattled against the house, and she knew that the leaves which had been so gorgeously yellow and red would be loosening their dying hold on their branches and swirling in to the corners of the garden. She had lived here now for over two years, and she knew that the house was snug and built to withstand the worst storms.

How her aunt had remonstrated with her! She was too young to shut herself away from the world — the fashionable world was what she meant — and there was talk that she had become eccentric and a bit of a bluestocking as well.

'You should be married.'

'One day. There is plenty of time.'

At this, her aunt threw up her hands in alarm.

'My dear, when I was your age, I was wed five years and had three daughters. With every year that passes, your chances decline. Now Tony is to be married before Christmas.'

'Ah, but my life has taken strange courses.'

A week after this discourse, she still felt unsettled. Forcing herself back to her task after glancing out of the window to see that her surmise about the leaves was correct, her chin set a little more firmly and her nib sputtered as her pen raced across the paper. The letter was almost a direct copy of one she had already written: to a wealthy neighbour asking whether it were possible that a place be found in his employ for a young lad, honest and of good disposition, whose father had died in Spain.

Lucius Stanton's request that she help Jemmy's family had led, she thought wryly, into others considering that she was a fairy godmother. As Jemmy's siblings had grown, she had found them places in turn, and she had thought was the end of it. However, Major Bretherton, amazed at her success, now drew to her attention the sorry plight of the family of a corporal who had served under him. Then a sergeant. Excellent fellows they had been, and not gaol sweepings.

Despite the good fire in the grate, she shivered. The Ogre, the Monster who had dominated Europe for so many years, had been finally vanquished at Waterloo in June that year, and for English Society, life had never been better. But, in England's humbler homes, victory already had a bitter and hollow sound.

The American war was over also, and as they did so often, and so hopelessly, her thoughts dwelled upon Lucius Stanton. It was a foolish exercise, she told herself sternly, and provided she kept on trying, she could forget him.

The sensible course would be to move out into Society for in the haute monde dominated by the Prince Regent, scandals were so plentiful that her own had long ago ceased to be of much interest. The new Lady Harley English and elegant, had made up her mind that her dear Anne must forget all this nonsense about playing Lady Bountiful. The past was past, and she should enjoy the pleasures to which her wealth and beauty entitled her, or better still, she could come to Paris to stay with them when Sir Emmet took up his new appointment there.

'Ah, but I fear that my cousin is quite determined to work out her own destiny.'

That was Sir Emmet speaking, distinguished, quite grey from the age of forty, gentler in his manner these days, although there was little in his appearance to indicate the torments he had endured as Anne, and the faithful valet recalled from exile, had helped him to fight his way back to health and reason. The drug, which Rosina had given him as a pretended remedy for his sleeplessness after the dreadful day when Inez had died, had soon made him its slave. A doctor who had had experience with opium addicts was discreetly summoned, and his advice was apparently simple. No matter how the patient begged, he must not be given the substance for which he craved.

Rosina, under pressure, admitted that the drug was derived from a plant chewed by Indians in the high Andes to give them relief from the difficulties of living in a rarified atmosphere. Anne found the supply hidden in the house and burnt it: that very night, Sir Emmet searched frantically for the drug, screaming and threatening to kill himself. As a fever reaches a crisis when the patient must fight or die, so it was for Sir Emmet Harley. After this, his will to conquer his addiction grew, and by the time Rosina and her brother came to trial for their assorted misdeeds, he was well enough to give evidence against them.

By the time he had fully recovered, Whitestairs was again its old, well-maintained self, and Anne had a house of her own where she had taken up residence accompanied by a circumspect and elderly relative from her mother's family, a Miss Sophie Snow.

Sir Emmet called on her one afternoon as

she was superintending a rearrangement of the garden. Although she lived only a short ride or drive from Whitestairs, they had not seen one another for some time, for Sir Emmet spent much time in London, trying to re-establish his career. Today he had news. There had been a resounding British victory in Spain, at Vittorio, and the French were in flight from Spain. This was not all he had to say.

'Are you sure,' he asked, as they went indoors, 'that this solitary life is what you want?'

'Emmet,' she responded, with a sigh, 'I wish only to live down my notoriety.'

He did not answer for a while, but stood by the window staring out at the garden.

'Anne,' he said, not looking at her, 'how can I make up for the wrongs I have done you? Everything was my fault. I began the tragedy when I married Inez because I wished to further my own fortunes. Not content with that, I prevented your marriage to Anthony Bretherton, and forced you to accompany us to Lima. Oh my God, Anne, there are times when I wish that you had permitted me to die!'

His outburst shocked her, all the more because of its truth, and yet at the same time, she was saddened to hear a proud and ambitious man talk thus.

'Emmet,' she said quietly, 'we can't undo what is done. As for Major Bretherton — my feelings for him were a silly school-girlish infatuation. He is a fine man, and I value his friendship, but I knew long ago that I did not really wish to marry him.'

'Would you marry me, Anne?'

Once again, she was astounded, and when she had recovered herself, she shook her head, smiling a little to help him through this difficult moment.

'No, Emmet. You were so very ill that I am quite sure no one would consider me compromised because I helped nurse you.'

'To give you my name,' he persisted, 'is the only way in which I can repair the damage I have caused in your bright young life.'

Tears flooded her eyes before she replied.

'Emmet, I have been cleared. Firstly, by the good offices of Mr. Lucius Stanton, and secondly by the confessions of that wretched Perez pair. I — I could not countenance a match where there was no depth of feeling. As for damage to my life — perhaps I learned something during my sufferings, Emmet. I see more. I understand more. I know that the whole world doesn't start and end within my own comfortable little circle.'

There was another long silence before he spoke.

'Anne, why didn't you come straight to me that day? Inez was my wife. It was my responsibility, not yours.'

She had to consider before answering, and when she did, it was not in direct reply.

'How well Rosina learned to understand us in a short time,' she said. 'I think she was sure that I would be the one to run to Robert Laurence's lodgings and thus compromise myself. But if I hadn't, and had called you instead . . . how cunning she was. There was no jewellery on Inez when I saw her lying dead. I would not be at all surprised if she intended flinging the whole blame on to her brother if you had gone instead of myself.'

Now that the object of his visit, a proposal of marriage, was over and done with, he was anxious to leave. But there was one thing more.

'Anne,' he said, taking her hand. 'Please allow me to at least attempt to make amends. There must be something I can do for you. Please.'

She realised that he must help to rid him of the enormous burden of guilt he carried. There was something she wished, and she told him what it was.

261

'I'll do what I can,' he promised, 'and if my attempts are successful — and I still have many powerful friends — you may be certain, Anne, that it will remain a secret between us always.'

Before the year was out, Sir Emmet Harley surprised everyone, including himself, by falling in love for the first time in his life. A marriage followed, which soon showed every sign of being a success.

Lucius Stanton wrote to Anne occasionally from the American side of the Atlantic. They were formal, proper letters, and vainly, she tried to read into them some indication that he regarded her as other than a friend. When Stanton had left England, she had been unashamedly downcast, and Major Bretherton, preparing for a return to Spain, had tried to console her.

'Fellow's as poor as a church mouse,' he had said. 'A fine old family, of course, but their fortunes foundered years ago. He's too proud to try for your hand.'

'I wish I were poor, too,' she cried, miserably.

'Fiddle faddle,' said the practical soldier. 'It's better by far to be rich and comfortable.'

So, on this afternoon in late 1815, as she tried to dedicate herself to her self-appointed task, she was very aware that she had to come to a decision. She was, after all, a perfectly normal young woman who longed for a husband and children of her own, but the years were slipping by, and she could see no reason why she could not combine good works with the fulfilment of her natural desires. Stanton's last letter had dashed what lingering hope she retained. He intended, he wrote, to take up land in New South Wales. Exploration had opened up new areas, and as he saw little future in a naval career now that the wars had ended, he intended to apply for the land grant to which he had become entitled as a serving officer. He had considered Canada, but he had formed a liking for New South Wales during his time there, and it was actually a far more pleasing place than many reports suggested. He knew that life there would not be easy for a start, but trying to achieve something there was preferable to accepting existence as a half-pay officer in his native England.

That was the end of that. Her nightmares about her ordeal on *The Eagle* were becoming less frequent, and so would eventually her dreams about the brave young man who had risked so much on her behalf. Only in silly romantic novels did heroes marry the damsels they had rescued. *That* was the stuff of childish fairy tales. She was foolish to have hoped otherwise.

Resolutely, she finished the letter she had been writing, and then drew a fresh sheet of paper towards herself.

'My dear Fanny,' she began, addressing the epistle to the present Lady Harley, 'I have been considering your kind suggestion that I join you in Paris when Emmet takes up his new appointment there, and I wish to say that I have decided that to live a while in Paris would be a most wonderful experience! You are absolutely right, Fanny. I have buried myself too long.'

She paused, and reflectively brushed the underside of her chin with the end of the quill. There was a smudge of ink on her middle finger, she noticed with a little burst of annoyance, and she was rubbing at this when the parlourmaid knocked and entered.

'Excuse me, Miss Stacey, but there's a gentleman asking to see you.'

'Oh dear, not the Reverend Mr. Williams again,' she said, half to herself. An excellent man in his way, but something of a bore, who preached that she cared too much for the material comfort of the poor and not enough for the patient resignation which would improve their souls and assure them of a place in a Better World. Anne thought this arrant rubbish, and knew that the time would come when she would find herself saying so.

'No, ma'am. He wouldn't give his name, but he asked me to repeat the word 'Botany' to you,' said the girl, looking very dubious about it.

'Botany!'

She did not bother about telling the girl to show in the visitor. She ran out into the entrance hall, noticing in a vague sort of way that Miss Sophie was coming downstairs, always eager for the ring of the doorbell, and cried out.

'Oh, Lucius! What a wonderful surprise!'

Then:

'How well you look!'

He was just a little heavier than formerly, and it suited him, giving him an air of authority which was almost instantly belied by the attractive smile she remembered so well, and that happy twinkle of brown eyes.

'And may I say the same of you, Miss Stacey.'

She had to introduce him to Miss Sophie, who was immediately all fluttering admiration, telling him how she had heard so much of the brave man who had gone to the aid of Anne when all had seemed lost.

He was a little taken aback at this, and Anne felt embarrassed that he should know how often she had spoken of him, but he smiled again and said that he had not actually gone to Miss Stacey's aid. He had been kidnapped whilst investigating a rumour, and had to make the best of things.

So he was taken in to warm himself by the fire, and offered tea, and complimented on coming so far out of his way to visit them. Miss Sophie was plainly entranced by this dashing caller, and then, tactlessly thought Anne, when they had all partaken of tea, announced that there must be matters which the young people wished to discuss together.

Anne's fair skin flamed, and as soon as the older woman had gone from the room, she turned to him.

'Pray take no notice of Miss Sophie. She is very much apt to jump to conclusions.'

'She is a very perceptive woman. I have been trying to catch her eye for the past ten minutes. Anne, she had helped me to come to the reason for my visit. I did not think that I should ever have the courage, nor the right, to ask, but will you come with me to New South Wales?'

It was so utterly unexpected that she could not say a word, and he spoke again, quickly.

'Perhaps I am assuming too much, but I saw Major Bretherton in London, and he gave me reason to hope. You see, dearest Anne, I am no longer completely penniless. Otherwise, I would not have dared offer for you. I am not very wealthy, of course, but now I have sufficient to build a house upon my land, and employ servants.'

'You wish me to become your wife?' Her voice was unsteady, for she could scarcely believe that such happiness was to be hers.

'Oh, what else could I wish? For so long it was an impossible dream. When I called upon you in London and saw the circumstances in which you lived, I knew that a poor naval officer could not presume, should not presume . . . '

Her hand slid across the small table to rest lightly on his strong tanned fingers.

'What cowardice,' she murmured, 'and from one who had been so brave.'

'You're a wonderful woman, Anne,' he said, and turned his hand palm upwards to twine his fingers through hers. 'Life will not be easy for us, at first, but you and I are alike, I think. We can both face difficulties, and even thrive on them.'

He arose from his own chair, and gently drew her to her feet, and their lips met, a little hesitantly at first, and then all restraint was thrown aside, and they clung to one another for a long time. At last, they separated, and stood quietly in the darkening room, watching the flames as she rested her head against his shoulder.

'To think,' he mused, stroking her fair hair, 'that the Golden Apostles have brought us together again, forever, my dearest one.'

He had been rewarded with prize money for his part in the recovery of the treasure, he said, a wonderful surprise which had awaited him on his return to England. A smaller amount had gone to Jemmy Thomas's mother.

So, Sir Emmet Harley had been as good as his word. Anne knew that it would remain a secret forever between him and herself that he had somehow convinced the rightful owners that Lucius Stanton should be recompensed for the recovery of that huge, shapeless mass of gold which had once been the Golden Apostles.

By so clearing his conscience, in part at least, the baronet had given her the chance of a happiness she had feared would never be hers.

We do hope that you have enjoyed reading this large print book.

Did you know that all of our titles are available for purchase?

We publish a wide range of high quality large print books including:
Romances, Mysteries, Classics
General Fiction
Non Fiction and Westerns

Special interest titles available in large print are:
The Little Oxford Dictionary
Music Book
Song Book
Hymn Book
Service Book

Also available from us courtesy of Oxford University Press:
Young Readers' Dictionary
(large print edition)
Young Readers' Thesaurus
(large print edition)

For further information or a free brochure, please contact us at:
Ulverscroft Large Print Books Ltd.,
The Green, Bradgate Road, Anstey,
Leicester, LE7 7FU, England.
Tel: (00 44) 0116 236 4325
Fax: (00 44) 0116 234 0205

Other books in the
Ulverscroft Large Print Series:

WHERE SHADOWS WALK

Angela O'Neill

Patrick Hegarty, elder son of farmer Joseph and Mary Ann, has no intention of carrying on the farming tradition. He sets off for Scotland to work with the navvies, but an encounter with a stone wall leaves him with a broken ankle. Nursed back to health by beautiful young Kate Kinard, the pair fall in love and are married without delay. But husband Patrick is a very different proposition from the romantic youth who courted her. The divide between them widens and Kate discovers that the saying 'Marry in haste, repent at leisure' may be more than just an old wives' tale . . .

THIS MORTAL COIL

Ann Quinton

'PETS. Exits arranged. Professionally. Effectively. Terminally. Apply: The Coil Shuffler.' Thus reads the business card of a professional assassin. When physiotherapist and lay reader Rachel Morland stumbles across one of these cards on the body of a frail parishioner, her suspicions are at once aroused, not least because she has seen it before — when her beloved husband apparently committed suicide. Policeman Mike Croft, a friend of Rachel's, also realises the significance of the calling-card and, together with his former boss, Nick Holroyd, sets out to track down the killer . . .

GRIANAN

Alexandra Raife

Abandoning her life in England after a broken engagement, Sally flees to Grianan, the beloved Scottish home of her childhood. Running Aunt Janey's remote country house hotel will be a complete break. Sally's brief encounter with Mike — gentle, loving but unavailable — cures the pain of her broken engagement, but leaves a deeper ache in its place. Caught up in the concerns of Grianan, Sally begins to heal. And when fate brings Mike into her life again, tragically altered, she has the strength and faith to hope that Grianan may help him too.

AN INCONSIDERATE DEATH

Betty Rowlands

In the sleepy Gloucestershire village of Marsdean, Lorraine Chant, wife of a wealthy businessman, is found strangled. But why, when both the Chants' safes had been discovered, was nothing stolen? What was Lorraine's relationship with Hugo Bayliss — a man with a dubious background and a penchant for attractive married women? How did Bayliss come to meet Sukey, police photographer and scene of crime officer, before the investigation became public? Then, in a cruel twist of fate, Sukey unwittingly plays into the hands of Lorraine's murderer . . .

THE SIMPLE LIFE

Lauren Wells

Lawrence Langland has had enough of corporate politics and fifteen-hour days. He wants out, to a simpler life. Isobel, his wife, whose gold-plated keyring says 'Born to Shop', has her own reasons for wanting to escape. Fortunately for Jacob, their eight-year-old son, it means leaving his horrible boarding school, although his elder sister Dory needs more persuading. And so the Langlands become 'downshifters', exchanging a comfortable house in suburbia for a small cottage in the countryside. Making the decision was the easy part — but can they cope with the reality?